CHILDREN
OF THE
SKY

Fran Adland.

SilverWood

Published in 2019 by SilverWood Books

SilverWood Books Ltd
14 Small Street, Bristol, BS1 1DE, United Kingdom
www.silverwoodbooks.co.uk

ISBN 978-1-78132-917-7 (paperback)
ISBN 978-1-78132-918-4 (ebook)

British Library Cataloguing in Publication Data
A CIP catalogue record for this book is available from
the British Library

Page design and typesetting by SilverWood Books
Printed on responsibly sourced paper

Children of the Sky is the second novel by award-winning author Fiona Holland. Her debut novel, *Before All Else*, was published in 2016. In 2013, Fiona won the Gladstone Library's Prize for Short Fiction and was runner-up in the 2017 Carnival of Words Literature Festival. Her short story *Listen Up!* was selected for public reading during the 2018 Daniel Owen Festival and *Traffic* is published by the University of Chester Press as part of their Cheshire Prize for Literature Anthology, *Island Chain*, in 2019.

Fiona is a creative writing tutor and runs a five-acre smallholding in North Wales.

For Nigel Johnson

Contents

CHILDREN OF THE SKY

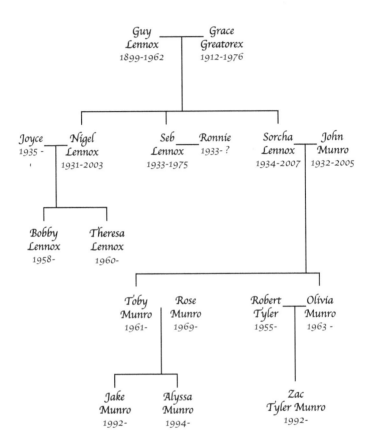

Chapter 1

August 2015

Olivia
Wellington, New Zealand

"It was never proven but there was always a suspicion that your Uncle Seb was murdered."

"Murdered?" Olivia tries to put down the cup of weak tea but the table is too far away, beyond her reach from the low sofa.

Had she heard right? Perhaps the last thirty-six hours of travelling to New Zealand from the UK, the sometimes unpredictable and sudden changes in altitude, the unfolding time zones, the hours of boredom, had affected her hearing or caused her mind to disfunction? Surely, nothing as grotesque – or glamorous, even – as a murder in the family had ever been mooted.

Aunty Joyce seems unwilling to pursue the topic and they return to staring at the same patch of worn out carpet underneath the portable gas heater in the centre of the room. Wind from the Antarctic blows over the Cook Strait and directly through ill-fitting windows into this sparse living room. Competing weather systems leave the room variously hot and cold. Olivia is cold.

They have been sitting here for half an hour since Joyce, her aunt distant in time, geography and family affiliation, had collected her from the airport and driven them to this far-flung suburb of Wellington. Switch-backing from side to side up the steep yellow-stone hillside; spiky flax and giant ferns waving them on. Road signs warned of flood, wind, earthquakes, landslides. Restless Maori *wairua* or spirits, perhaps.

Eleven thousand miles and they seem to have very little to say to each other. Kezia, the overweight Maltese terrier, eyes her malevolently from under the coffee table as if also asking herself the question, what is she actually doing here, so far from home?

Olivia's phone pings. Zac. "Hi Mum." Aunty Joyce looks up from the patch of carpet. "It's Zac. Texting to say he'll be here in half an hour." Joyce nods. Olivia would pirouette round this small, shabby living room with the joy of seeing her only-born son for the first time in six months, but Joyce's tightly clenched lips don't encourage gaiety.

Would it, in the meantime, be unseemly to redirect Joyce's attention back to Uncle Seb? Seb. Anarchic. A dropout. A loner. But loaded with glamour and mystique. And so at odds with and so unlike her own mother, Sorcha, that any brother or sister could be. Was he really *murdered*?

Maybe Joyce is feeling the strain of making conversation with her niece whom she has not seen for thirty years. A virtual stranger. Who is now sitting in her living room. Olivia had been surveying the objects in the room – some carved wooden figures, African or Maori she couldn't tell, a few books that look like text books, some heavy-handed oils on the walls. She should stop looking with quite such curiosity for fear that it might look like acquisitiveness. After all, how would she feel in Joyce's position?

Perhaps they should put Seb aside for a moment until the more routine pleasantries are out of the way.

"So, I understand Uncle Nigel was really young when he emigrated to New Zealand." Joyce looks melancholy. Her eyes flicker to a small photograph of her husband on the mantlepiece. A man in his forties. Red jacket. Pale blue studio background. Olivia would like to take a closer look but the low-slung, thinly-upholstered sofa holds her at bay.

"Yes. Seventeen. One of the ten pound Poms."

Seventeen. Extraordinarily young to be making the one-way trip. Was he running to something or away from something? Towards adventure, self-discovery, opportunity? Or had there been some other less salubrious reason for going? Was it his decision to go, or had the decision been made for him? The questions whirl round Olivia's mind.

"That really is so young. I think of Zac, at twenty-two, making this trip and get anxious. It would have been so different – what – nearly seventy years ago."

"It is a good thing for boys to leave their mothers. Zac will be better for it." Joyce's tone is matter of fact, making no concessions to Olivia's maternal fears. "It was by far the best thing for Nigel."

"Oh?"

"Yes. Most definitely."

Olivia looks straight at her aunt – eighty if she's a day, brisk, toned, her chin-length bob straight and glossy, her eyes raptor-sharp – willing her to speak. Joyce seems disinclined to say more, jaw clamped shut. Perhaps it is only a question of finding the right way in.

"So, how did you and Nigel meet?"

Here Joyce laughs. "We met the way most people used to meet their future spouses. At work. We were both working for the Public Works Department. Nigel was in town planning, I was in housing. There were some local protests in Johnsonville about plans for a highway that would have cut across Maori tracks from the hinterland to an ancient settlement on the coast. We both gave evidence to the District Commissioner's inquiry. It was all just politics really. Nobody was that bothered about native rights back then. Different nowadays. Anyway, Nigel invited me out to dinner. I had no idea where he was from. Had no sense he was British because he'd spent so much time out in Rhodesia when he was young. Had this peculiar hybrid accent. Sort of colonial equivalent to a mid-Atlantic accent. But he was charming, and polite."

"And he won you over."

"He did, after a while. I felt sorry for him. Didn't know what to do with him. He looked out of place. Had a sort of faraway pioneering look in his eye. I told him that, as a nation, we were doing just fine thank you. That there was no need to go about looking to quell or improve the natives. Once we'd got that sorted out and he'd settled down, we got on just fine. Married in 1955. Bobby and Theresa were born within five years."

"I knew Mum grew up in Rhodesia and she hated it out there. I didn't realise that Uncle Nigel was there too. I assumed that, like Seb, he'd been sent to boarding school back in the UK."

"No. He was out there with Sorcha, your Mum, and their parents Guy and Grace. He said that Rhodesia didn't suit Sorcha. That she was frightened by the heat and the intensity and the strangeness of the place. She was better suited to cooler tones; a more muted palette. Marrying your father was the right thing for her. He sheltered her. Although we were a little surprised when you and Toby came along."

Olivia feels a curious tremor, as if she and her brother Toby were not quite so non-negotiable as the very fact of their existence would seem to make them.

Joyce rises swiftly from her seat, muttering, "I've got photographs," before leaving the room.

The walls are clad with wood-effect plastic panels. Tacked here and there are the oil paintings that had earlier caught her eye. Olivia struggles off the sofa to take a closer look. They are scenes she recognises. St Paul's Cathedral, the London sky pigeon-grey behind its illuminated dome. What looks like Salisbury Cathedral, its tall, delicate spire not quite true, rudimentary figures playing cricket on a green in the foreground. She moves around the room. Here a larger canvas. Children sitting on a low brick wall eating icecream, a bicycle, Stop Me and Buy One, nearby. The work has a nostalgic air, as if the artist were looking for totems of a more secure age.

Olivia stares at the paintings. There are gaps between the canvases and the crude, white wooden frames. Brown tape curls its way between the wall and a painting, like a creeping rhizome. If lifted down off their hooks, they would surely fall apart in her hands, the rusting staples working free.

"They were painted by your grandmother, Grace, once the family returned from Rhodesia in the late 1950s. Nigel asked for them when she died. I hate the bloody things." Aunty Joyce has come back in the room, a slatted wooden box in her hand. "They show all the mistakes of the amateur painter. Perspective's all wrong and the colours too gaudy. Fey! But Nigel wanted them. I've just never got round to taking them down now…now he's dead."

Joyce holds the small box to her lap, arms braced over it as if not quite ready to allow the contents to escape. On the side of the orange crate is stencilled the name E.G. Fillarkey, Grocers, Mombasa.

There is another painting by the kitchen door, dimly lit by the central bulb hanging from the ceiling. It's a bright, abstract canvas. Red, orange, black. "This one's quite good," Olivia offers, turning towards Joyce. "It's got a title. I can't really read it."

"Kopje. K.o.p.j.e. pronounced 'koppie'. A small, stony hillside. African."

"Did Grace paint this one? It looks quite different. Much more assured. More accomplished."

"No. That was actually painted by a friend of your mother's. She told me about him in one of her Christmas letters. They met at art school in Liverpool in the seventies. She sent this painting over when she sent her mother's paintings. She called it an unnecessary and unwarranted gift, one she hadn't felt inclined to accept. Not sure if she wanted me to think the artist was her lover." Joyce pauses to study Olivia. "Don't look at me like that. Things happen."

"Well, not to my mother they didn't."

"I don't know. She was always very oblique, your mother."

Oblique, certainly. With very clear opinions that divorce and extramarital affairs lead to nothing but shame and penury. Lucky for her she married such an honourable man. Not so lucky for Daddy, perhaps.

Joyce is clutching a packet of letters. "These are all the letters I received from your mother. Every Christmas and every birthday. Until of course…"

"Yes, of course."

"Letters here spanning nearly six decades. I can't let you read them, you understand."

"No. Of course not."

16

But why the secrecy? Had Sorcha allowed a few fragments of herself to dislodge into these annual letters and fly across the oceans? Could Aunty Joyce offer some insight into the working of Sorcha's mind? Why she was so indifferent to her children? Why to Olivia and Toby she was at best neglectful, at worst cruel?

How very odd to find herself sitting in a virtual stranger's house on the other side of the world. A stranger unrelated by blood, related only by a series of circumstances that began when Uncle Nigel left Rhodesia as such a young man and so long ago.

How very odd that this remote stranger could see deeper into her family than she could ever know. Maybe this was another reason for her visit, unexpressed until now.

"Here's a picture of your mother. Taken around the time of Seb's wedding. She'd have been around eighteen or nineteen then."

Olivia takes the large black and white photograph, the mount thick between her fingers. Brown spots mottle the white margins. "She…is…so…beautiful," Olivia whispers, stiffening herself to unfavourable comparison. Her mother is gazing slightly off to the left. Her dark hair is cut short, gamine-style, sharp points lying on her high cheeks, framing delicately whorled ears and large eyes. One hand is placed on her cheek and she is grasping the wrist of the other hand. The pose is studied, artful, adding to her simple, unadorned beauty. An unnatural beauty. An undeserved beauty.

"And this is Nigel. You never met him, unfortunately."

"Yes, that is a shame." Olivia studies his face closely for family resemblance. His eyes are serious, intelligent, slightly distrusting perhaps. Joyce removes the photograph from Olivia's hands and tucks it down beside her. "I wish I'd known him."

"Yes. So do I. I think you would have liked each other."

Joyce hands Olivia the third photograph. "Seb."

She remembers Seb, but very differently to this young, whip-thin, clean-shaven bridegroom standing on the steps of a brick municipal building, looking sidelong at a small, pared-down woman in a sheer, wide-brimmed hat and floor-length white cotton dress. "Is this Seb's wife?"

"Yes. Ronnie. They married shortly after the family returned from Rhodesia."

"I don't know if I ever met Ronnie."

"No. It didn't last."

"Magda? I might have met Magda, when they visited once?"

"Ha! Yes, your mother wrote about Magda. She didn't like her one bit. Blamed her for what happened to Seb." Might Joyce tell her how Seb changed from the fresh-faced young man in this picture to the roving, unkempt yet strangely alluring visitor to the family home when she and Toby were young, to possibly being murdered? Had he come to their house to ask for money? Had Sorcha, who had never given her or Toby a single sou, felt obliged to pay Seb? "But that, as they say, *is* for another time. I can see your son arriving."

A white camper van swings onto the drive. Zac slides out of the driver's seat. The last time Olivia had seen him, on Skype, he had looked tired, travel-worn, ill-nourished. He'd been puzzled, angry even, that she wanted to fly all the way to New Zealand. She was worried about him. But couldn't tell him that. Luckily the digital picture had pixelated itself into a cubist montage before cutting out completely and ending the conversation. Over the next few weeks while she prepared for the trip, Zac asked no further questions.

She takes a few moments to watch him from the window before going out to greet him. He *is* thin, she mutters to herself, taking in the looseness of his clothes. He removes his earphones and circles the wires round his fingers before neatly stowing them in a pocket. He fusses with his shirt and jeans. How like your father, she groans. He looks up and catches her watching through the window. He waves.

"Go on. Let him in."

Olivia opens the front door. "Over here," she shouts. Zac drops his large rucksack and scoops her into a hug. They hold each other for a long minute.

Really it had been a bitch asking Toby for money for the trip, but he was the only person she knew who had any. A sharp, gleeful look had flashed across his face. "What, short of funds then, Sis? Not managing terribly well?" She'd instantly halved the amount she was going to ask for, preferring to try her luck with the credit card company than suffer Toby's patronage. "Can't you ask your latest conquest for money?"

"Hadley? He's got no money."

"No, they never do, do they?"

Finally, Toby had consented to lend her enough for the airfare, but there had been conditions. Yes, she promised she would take a long hard look at herself. Yes, she knew that the usual palliatives of food, sex, booze had put her on a completely destructive path. Yes, she knew that Mummy and Daddy wouldn't approve. Yes, sir. No, sir. Money-bags-full, sir.

Later that night, Zac offers to cook supper. Kezia lies patiently, a line of drool glistening on her crossed paws. Joyce is sitting with a glass of sherry. Olivia tries lemonade.

Zac sings tunelessly but happily and clatters and bangs his way round the kitchen. Joyce is irritated. "I think it's more than just childishness men bring with them into adulthood."

"Oh." There is caution in Olivia's voice. "What else?"

"Anger. The sort of anger that goes with being thwarted. By events or their own failings." Joyce shoots a look into the kitchen. "I don't think Zac's got it. Nigel didn't have it. But there is a streak of something in your family. A temper."

Olivia thinks back to her conversation with Toby. Yes, Toby has a kind of harsh anger about him. Daddy? No, not Daddy. He was gentle.

Joyce is talking again. "You can pick out the ones with this unnatural fire – the ones that will burn you if you get too close."

Seb, perhaps? Joyce still hasn't told her his story. Maybe she doesn't just mean the male members of the family. Sorcha? Oh, most definitely Sorcha. And what of Sorcha's parents – Grace and Guy?

"Apparently it takes seven generations for the effects of a trauma to work its way through a family. It's like a black fire. It doesn't burn everyone, but those it burns do suffer. They become the black fruits."

As Zac calls them through to eat, Olivia wonders just which members of the family are the black fruits.

Chapter 2

May 1931

Grace
Liverpool

She stands sidelong to the cheval mirror, her belly pushing outwards. Guy is hoping for a boy. Nigel, they will call him. Nigel Lennox. At last they have found rooms of their own. Three attic rooms where the walls slope upwards to a point. Like being in a pyramid. They cannot stay here, in her childhood bedroom, within its sprigged wallpaper walls. A married woman's bed is a very different place.

In the quiet pause before they have to get going, she thinks back to when she first met Guy. She had been standing on the Pier Head, waiting for the ferry, aware of his glances as she threw bread to the wheeling gulls. The wind funnelling down the Mersey had snatched away his first words to her.

"Sorry. I didn't catch that." The wind tugged at her hair and her head scarf.

"Vermin. You're feeding vermin."

How appropriate that his first words to her were about vermin and hers contained an apology.

He had carried on talking but she couldn't really hear what

he was saying above the clamour of the overhead railway, the trams and the porters. He had an authority about him, even then. She was to become a moon to his planet. His words went scudding over the wavelets of the brown Mersey. Despite the blustery weather, a delicate mist was forming and tiny droplets took roost in his moustache. She caught the words 'émigré' and 'dispossessed'. He must have been talking about his work. She imagined him gallantly handing down a Russian Countess from a first-class railway carriage, her jewels stitched safely within the seams of her cloak. Or was that a little fanciful? It later turned out he had been on secondment from the Foreign Office in London, investigating the asylum claims of refugees flung upon these chilly British shores following the War.

They both joined the press of people boarding the ferry for Birkenhead. Smoke from the funnel mixed with the pearls of sea mist, smudging the view of the emerging ventilation towers for the road tunnel on the other shore. He'd asked about her work. "I work in the Tax Office. I live in New Brighton." What more was there to say about herself?

The ferry, fighting against the tides and contrary winds, jibbed and bucked and she struck her forehead on his shoulder. "Oh, I am most dreadfully sorry. Are you hurt?" he asked. He placed a hand on her shoulder and scanned her face as if, only at that precise moment, he'd become aware of her features, her youthfulness, her self.

"I'm fine." Despite tears threatening to flood the rims of her eyes, she repeated, "Fine." He turned away from her and she watched a large droplet of water fall from a rusted railing on the upper deck and land on the shoulder of his woollen coat. A small detail. A small, unnoticed, irrelevant detail but, looking back, it seemed to mark a point when her life began marshalling those small things while the man she stood next to looked out over wider vistas.

Before they married, he'd told her that they too would emigrate one day. Start a new life.

She feels but a child. Nineteen. He is older. Thirty-two. In their short marriage, she has already learned a valuable lesson, not to mistake his impassivity for lack of resolve. She shudders at her early naivety.

He likes Grace to go on top. She knows herself to be slim-waisted. He loves the roundness of her heavy buttocks as she opens wide to let him in. The wider she spreads, the tighter she becomes. "Arch your back," he commands, pulling her knees further apart across the rumpled bed sheet. She feels she might split in two. She is dry and the position feels unnatural, as if his penis is kinked inside her. It feels like the bulbous end is jutting up against bone even though, logically, this is probably impossible.

"Darling," she'd whispered, as much to take her mind from the discomfort of her lower quarters as to coax his attention.

She'd been astonished the first time she'd seen him reach orgasm. The way his face changes. Almost a completely different face, fragmented, the features, the colouring re-arranging into a different man's.

His mouth was opening wide, his lips pulling tight over his teeth. He was obviously close.

She coughed and spoke again, "Darling," this time a bit louder. Had he heard her? Perhaps this wasn't really the best time.

His eyelids began their flutter. He grasped her hips, lifting her into the air, allowing a precious release of the almost unbearable strain in her hips. He starts to slap her as a jockey might with only one more furlong to go, until it penetrates his consciousness that his wife is talking to him. Once she'd started, it seemed senseless to stop. She just hoped the family couldn't hear them through the thin walls of her bedroom.

He lowered them both back down to the bed. His features rearranged themselves back into something more recognisably Guy's. His eyes focussed on her face, her mouth, as she began her spiel. "I know we talked about it a couple of days ago, but I really do feel that if we don't go back to the estate agents and tell them that we're interested in that flat, then someone else might get it, and it really is perfect for us."

"I don't fucking believe you!" he'd gasped. She was roughly shoved over to the other side of the bed, a quick onset of tears prickling her eyes. Really, properties in this part of the city get snapped up ever so quickly. Why can't he see that what she's saying makes perfect sense?

"I'm…sorry…" She wanted to reach out to Guy now sitting on the edge of the bed, fingers running through his still thick and abundant hair. "I…didn't…realise."

"You stupid fucking cow. Don't ever do that again." He stood and walked towards the door. In the mirror she could see his erection, still thick, shiny, magenta. He stomped down the landing to the bathroom. A sharp crash, as if he had swiped the contents off the bathroom shelf, followed by softer, muted moans. Ten minutes later he returned to the marital bed. She pretended to be asleep, uncovered, having left him the blankets and eiderdown in both apology and hope that he might rediscover his tenderness and re-cover her. Which he didn't.

For days after her early faux pas, Guy barely spoke to her. Eventually, on the sixth night, he did pull the covers over her shoulder, kissing the nape of her neck. She turned and flung her arms round his neck in deep and tearful and pathetic gratitude. They hadn't got that flat; perhaps it was for the best.

She knows now, in the face of Guy's granite resolve, neither persistence or petulance cut any ice. She knows what she must do. Her silence will match his silence. Her patience will match his. She will wait. She will outwait even Guy.

For now, now they have got their own rooms, she will leave her family home and await the baby.

Chapter 3

August 1947

Grace
Salisbury, Rhodesia

The houseboys are leaving work, shouting farewell to the cook-boy who is, hopefully, preparing something for the children's tea. Dusk is drawing in and, from the balcony, she can hear the clink clink of chains jumping over gears, the screech of hot rubber bicycle tyres, the quiet susurration of the black workers hurrying to leave Salisbury on their bicycles for their villages before the curfew starts. Guy isn't home yet from work.

Once he has prepared the children's tea, Jacob will hunker in his shed at the bottom of the garden waiting Guy's return and the order to serve dinner. She has never visited the ramshackle arrangement of sheds that house the street's workers. They are rudimentary, barely habitable but run on far more communal lines than the neat row of discrete, sweltering concrete bungalows built for the colonial workforce. Bougainvillea and hibiscus tumble over the random lines of the sheds and glow with colour and fragrance.

"School's boring," Sorcha sighs. Grace watches with detachment as Sorcha scores deep lines into the flimsy wooden table with her colouring pencils. "These pencils are no good either." Despite Sorcha's persistence, the colours on the rough, fibrous paper remain muted, unsatisfactory.

"Careful, darling. You'll go through the paper."

"Don't care."

"That's no way to speak."

"Sorry."

"Sorry…?"

"Sorry, Mummy."

Grace looks at her thirteen-year-old daughter sitting on her heels, doggedly trying to fill in the outlines of her colouring book.

"Nkumbe had a snake in a box in his car today." Nigel walks in and starts juggling with oranges from the fruit bowl.

"Don't do that, Nigel. Put the oranges back."

"Did you hear me, Mummy? Nkumbe said he had a green mamba that someone from his village had found in a pile of pumpkins. He said he would keep it as a pet and train it to guard the car when he left it to go to the market. He said he would leave it under the windscreen where it would like the heat and warn everyone not to steal the car because he would train it to bite thieves."

Grace looks at her son, so earnest, returning his insistent gaze, testing the truth of his words, drawing the truth from him like venom. "Honestly, Mummy."

"I really don't think he would be allowed to have a snake in the school car, darling. But I will have a word with Miss Scott about it tomorrow."

"No, Mummy, you mustn't. He made me promise not to tell anyone."

"So, why did you?" pipes up Sorcha.

"I…don't…know."

Sorcha clamps her lips together and concentrates on a small area of colour on the page.

Grace isn't sure whether to pursue this line of enquiry and let Nigel naturally expose himself as a liar or whether to just let the whole matter rest. Really, the hour between the children coming home from school and their evening meal being prepared can be quite trying. "Well, I'm sure it would be a very friendly snake if indeed snake it is." She tries for diplomacy and wishes Nigel would just go and find something to occupy himself with.

"I saw it too, Mummy." Sorcha puts down her pencils. "It was yellow."

A tinkling sounds from inside the house. It is Jacob's signal that the children's food is ready. "Come on, children, let's go and eat."

Sorcha places each pencil in turn in the shallow tin while Nigel flicks an orange off his upper arm towards the fruit bowl. It misses and rolls under the sideboard. One year in Rhodesia and Nigel has learned that there is always someone to follow on behind to pick up the discards. She imagines the orange slowly shrivelling against the skirting board over the next few days. She might tell him to pick it up but is sure that he will refuse.

"Come along, Sorcha. Hurry up with those pencils. Your meal will be getting cold."

Grace sits alongside the children in the gloomy dining room as they pick at their strange food. She smokes three cigarettes in turn, careful to blow the smoke out of the open window, while ash peppers the oilcloth. At her elbow, yet another polite request from Sorcha and Nigel's school that their account be settled with all due promptitude. No letters have arrived from Seb for at least three weeks. Afterwards they will sit down together and write their weekly letter to him. At least he had the brains and the good fortune to get a scholarship to the Portsmouth naval academy, and avoid being dragged to this god-forsaken outpost.

There has been so much to get used to in the last twelve months since the family moved to Rhodesia. She wonders if they really aren't a bit too old to start anew. Guy, at forty-seven, isn't he past the point of being the pioneer, the frontier man, the adventurer he sees himself?

Married for almost half her life now and all through her marriage she has lived with Guy's ambition, his restlessness, his need to prove himself. Do they really have a chance of a better life here?

It would have been unpatriotic, not to say impossible, for them to leave while the war was on. When it was over, she had wanted to stay at home. Join the push, brick by brick, for reconstruction. She hadn't minded the post-war austerity, the reduced rations. She had felt exhilarated. There was enough food to feed her young family. They were part of a bright future.

The war hadn't ended with the declaration of peace. There was another war – against intolerance, Fascism, invasion and occupation – still to be fought. But what mattered in Europe matters little here. Her concerns are not Guy's concerns.

Guy spoke of Rhodesia as a seedbed for all the old principles and virtues that had somehow become corrupted. The world needed to rekindle the old values, go back to the frontiers of individualism, enterprise, every man for himself. The lessons of the war, the way of the war – community, commonality, socialism even – they were just so much pernicious propaganda.

Just before they left Liverpool, she had visited the Tropical House in Sefton Park. How muted and undernourished the exotic plants had seemed; the flowers like much of her city of Liverpool, pinched and faded in the post-war gloom.

But she is here now. They might as well make the best of it. At least the flowers are lovely.

The front door slams as she is tucking the children into their beds. Guy is home.

"Night, night children." She kisses them quickly before hurrying downstairs.

"Jacob! Jacob! Come here, damn you." Guy is leaning out over the balcony and shouting into the falling darkness. There is no answer from the bottom of the garden although an orange light flickers between the boards of the shed. Dark shapes move here and there, throwing elongated shadows out into the thick night air. Sounds of laughter and gossip rise and fall, wave after wave.

"You know what's going on, don't you? He's robbing us blind. We're feeding him and half his bloody village."

"I'm not sure that's right…"

"They'd take food from your plate faster than a rat can roll a stolen egg."

"Darling…!"

"Where's that bloody whisky?" Guy goes along the kitchen cupboards opening and slamming each door in turn. "Where's that bloody boy?"

"Come and sit and I'll find you some." Grace gestures towards Guy's chair.

"Be quick about it."

Grace catches Jacob in the corridor. "Jacob," she whispers. "Where's the master's whisky?" Is there the merest glimpse of panic in the black boy's eyes? Did he remember to replenish the drinks cabinet? There will be hell to pay if he has forgotten. Has he, in fact, stolen the whisky? God forbid.

"I find whisky, ma'am." It is with relief that she watches Jacob walk over to the drinks trolley. Not for the first time does she observe how he, and others like him, walk in a different rhythm to the Europeans – a sort of loose-limbed, linear waltz, three beats to the white man's two. "I am sorry, ma'am. It is here all along." He points to the trolley and the bottles of spirit. The whisky is where it always is.

"Thank you, Jacob. I'll take it to him." He places the glass onto a small, circular silver-dipped tray. She picks the glass up from the tray, careful not to touch Jacob's fingers.

She hands Guy his drink; he is wreathed in cigarette smoke. Mosquitoes hover an inch or two above floor height. She watches as one lands on the small band of white flesh above his sock cuff. She might feel obliged to shoo it away but takes a quiet delight in leaving it to do its work.

"Here you are, darling. Whisky." She will have to wait for the drink to take effect before she tackles the subject of the as yet unpaid school bills, and so picks up her embroidery. Darkness is falling fast. The light from the dim bulbs cuts out.

"Bloody electricity supply. What's wrong now?" Guy rises stiffly from his chair to peer out of the window. "Whole bloody district's off. Can't they organise themselves a bit better or is it the bloody mob sabotaging the supply again?"

She might ring for Jacob to light the hurricane lamps but this would only delay supper. She folds her sewing into her lap and watches Guy's dark bulk against the grey of the night.

"Guy?" she calls out tentatively. His gaze is fixed on the veld below the sprawl of newly built bungalows. Has he heard her? She walks slowly from the soft gloom of the sitting room onto the veranda. The soft red earth is sandy beneath the wooden slats. Here and there, shadows fill the indentations, a hand's span across, where the hens took their rest today. Implausibly, a green, fleshy, ground-covering plant pushes its way out from under the veranda. She places a hand on his arm, the letter in her other hand. "We need to talk about some household bills."

Guy doesn't answer. He stands solid, unmoving. She feels pinioned. Trapped. If she removes her hand, it might signal to Guy that the conversation is at an end. She continues to stand by his side, careful not to let her hand grow heavy or tremble against his arm. An airplane lifts off in the distance at the far side of the city towards the reddening horizon. Guy is implacable. Why the blazes had she married such a difficult man? She almost feels sorry for him.

She would like to ask if they are short of money. If there is some difficulty with paying the school bill. Or is it just an oversight on his part? Had he even heard her? His jaw tightens; his back teeth grind. Can they even afford the school fees?

The lights pop back on and the hum and grumble of generators die down. Guy makes his way over to the drinks trolley.

Grace picks up her embroidery and leaves Guy to his third whisky before Jacob appears at the door to tell them that dinner is ready. Guy remains in his seat, forearms resting on the wooden arms of the chair, the drink in his hand at a forty-five-degree angle. Has he heard Jacob? Grace signals to the man to repeat himself, only louder. Jacob stands in the doorway, his white-gloved hands crossed in front of him, and coughs. "Ma'am. Sir. Dinner is served."

"I heard you the first time, man," Guy explodes. Jacob stands back slightly as Grace edges towards the door but Guy is still immobile.

"Come along, now, darling. Don't be awkward. Jacob is waiting to serve dinner." She holds out her hand as if to lift him from his chair. He pushes her roughly away. Jacob lets out a muffled protest. Come on, Guy; the silent prayer fills her mind. We don't want a showdown tonight. Let's just go in and eat our dinner and let Jacob go home, then you can sleep it off. Whatever it is won't seem so bad in the morning.

A sigh escapes her chest, unexpectedly, before she can mute it. Guy's head swivels round to stare at her. His nostrils are wide, his breathing fast and loud. He lets out an inarticulate roar before rising quickly to his feet, throwing the whisky glass against the wall. "Don't…you…bitch…" Words, disjointed, unconnected, force their way between his clenched teeth. "What do you fucking care about…?" His eyes are locked on Grace's as he picks up a glass ashtray from the table.

"Guy…" Grace backs away, holding out one hand to repel him. "Guy! Stop this now." He is like a bull, dense, snorting, blind with rage. Grace feels herself pulled to one side as Jacob inserts himself before Guy. Guy punches him on the cheekbone. Once. Twice. Three times. There is no fear in Jacob's eyes, only defiance and hatred. She wants Jacob to hit him back. Hard. But knows he won't. Guy leans his arm up the wall. There is a trickle of rich blood coming from Jacob's lower lip. A purple bloom spreads across his cheek. Jacob slips away and she hears a commotion from the huts at the bottom of the garden. How safe will they be in their beds tonight? She turns her back on Guy and walks wearily to the bedroom. The ants can eat their supper.

Two days later, the family walk through Belvedere Park after Church. She buys the children an ice cream each from the pavilion. When she looks again, Sorcha is standing stiffly, awkwardly, runnels of ice cream dripping from her outstretched tongue. She hurries forward to wipe the mess from her daughter's tongue, chin, hair, coat. "What's wrong, darling?" She anxiously checks for insects or broken glass, for blood. Guy looks on from the shade of a maple tree, shaking a cigarette free from its packet. As Sorcha yells, she hears the click as Guy flips the lid of his chrome lighter.

"It's off! The ice cream is off!"

Nigel runs his tongue in a helter-skelter round his own ice cream. "No, it's not. It's fab!" She glances at him caught between the competing forces of mocking his younger sister and licking back the fast-melting surface of his ice cream to a cooler layer beneath.

"It's not off. You've got the same as Nigel. His is alright."

"It tastes funny." Sorcha proffers her the cone.

"No, you eat it, darling. It's not off."

"It is. It is. It is."

Nigel, seizing his opportunity, gulps the remainder of his ice cream, folding the soggy cone into four before stuffing it into his mouth. "I'll have it if you don't want it."

"No, you bloody don't!" Guy steps forward and grabs the offending mess from Sorcha, throwing his part-smoked cigarette at Grace's feet, wisps of smoke twisting upwards.

Mutely, the ice cream vendor holds out his own hands to accept the dripping mass from Guy's. "I am afraid that my daughter is too good for your ice cream."

"Thank you, sir. I am very sorry to hear that."

The small party turn to watch Guy stride off to a nearby water fountain to wash his hands, drying them on an extravagant handkerchief. Grace stoops to usher the children and extinguish the discarded cigarette with the point of her shoe. "I'm terribly sorry about that."

"Ma'am." The ice cream vendor, red and white striped hat and apron immaculate, stands stock-still, ice cream still dripping through his long, dark fingers, as if protocol will not allow him to take action until the family rapidly fracturing in front of him has moved on.

"Come along, children. After Daddy."

"Well, you lost out there, didn't you? Idiot!"

"Nigel. Stop taunting your sister."

"It tasted horrid."

"Sorcha. Quiet. Quickly now." If they don't hurry, Guy will make off for the Club or some inner-city bar, leaving them to make their own way home and she hasn't the money for a taxi.

How quickly children prise their wanton fingers into every fissure, guilelessly showing up every crack, every fault in a marriage. She tugs on their slender arms, pulling them along behind her, some of Guy's anger filling her veins, Sorcha crying, Nigel laughing. She feels her own heat rising. It would be hours now before Guy's anger dissipates and Sorcha stops her juddering tears. Oh, Christ, just what is she supposed to do here?

Nigel says something.

"What did you say?"

"I said it probably tasted funny because they use buffalo milk here."

"Buffalo! Ooooh, Mummy! That's disgusting!"

"Or bison."

"Nigel. Quiet."

"Or elephant or zebra."

"Muuummy," Sorcha wails, her feet tripping over themselves so that she is part dangling from Grace's arm, her knees threatening to scrape along the path.

"Nigel. Shut up!"

When they get home, Jacob is gone and a stranger calls at the back door for the thick envelope Guy has left on the kitchen windowsill.

Chapter 4

June 1951

Grace
Ad Astra Club, Heaney Airfield
Salisbury, Rhodesia

Guy had told her to wait for him in the Lounge. All being well, he would be along at around 6.30, provided the procurement meeting between the Air Vice Marshall and the mandarins from London didn't run on too long. It is now ten past seven, Grace has been waiting for nearly an hour and she is desperate for a drink. The telephone on the end of the long zinc bar rings. She watches the steward answer, in case it is Guy sending his regrets, telling her to get a drink or to dine on her own or to meet him elsewhere. The steward does not catch her eye so she returns to the fashion magazine on her lap, its softened pages already several months out of date and a world away.

The night air is cooling. Someone has switched off the overhead fans and the lace points of her blouse's collar and the magazine pages cease their restlessness. The crowd of instructors from the Flight Training School move from their positions at the bar, where they have been loudly ordering beer and brandy, to take up three of the low tables directly behind her. An elbow nudges her. Unable to see who apologises, she nonetheless feels herself redden as, after a brief pause in the chatter, the group laughs collectively. She touches the back of her neck with her gloved hand. Again, she glances at the steward as if he might rescue her from this entrapment, this indecision. For, if she stands up now, she would be in full view of the air crew, an uneasy and unwilling target for their jocularity. To stay seems the only, if uncomfortable, option.

The smell of the cheap local beer and the French brandy make her even more desperate for a drink. If Guy doesn't arrive in the next ten minutes, she will go home and suffer the consequences.

The bar lounge fills up – bureaucrats from the government offices on St James Street, flying recruits, women from the air auxiliary and their partners for the evening. Pairs in their tennis whites walk in off the terraces, standing close, leaning their free hands on the empty seat backs around her table. A palisade of people around her, Rumpelstiltskin. Would Guy even find her now?

The crowd parts as Alfonso, the Club manager, approaches her. He leans forward to whisper in her ear, the jug of iced water hovering perilously near the edge of the round tray supported on his backward-turned hand. "May I escort Madam to the library? I fear that you may be somewhat incommoded here."

Someone like Kitty would laugh in his face and tell him not to be such an old bigot, that she has every right to take up a seat, five seats, if she so wishes, and that if he doesn't like a single woman sitting on her own, well then he should jolly wake up to the modern age. Grace is not Kitty though. Grace lacks Kitty's bravado and gutsiness, and meekly and gratefully follows the diminutive man's white jacket and black, glistening hair to the furthest corner, laughably called 'The Library'.

Beneath the tooled red and gold leather bound Collected Works of Dickens sits a man. She takes a seat at the furthest end of the banquette, as guided by Alfonso, and gratefully accepts the jug of iced water. Being round the corner from the bar, the area has a backstage feel to it – dark, dusty, all the action taking place elsewhere. Yellow light from the shaded lamps in the centre of the tables casts a mellow glow. She wonders if the man in the corner has enough light to read by and what he is reading.

This man fails to look up or acknowledge her presence. She sips her water, watching the ice cube slide up and down inside the frosted glass, like the air bubble in a spirit level. Vodka would have been nice but it would have been beyond her to ask for some.

How long is Guy going to be?

After a few minutes, her silent companion unbuttons the top pocket of his khaki shirt, removing a packet of Players and a steel lighter. Absent-mindedly, he places a cigarette in his mouth before pulling out another and offering it to her. She slides it out from beneath his thumb and looks into his eyes as he leans over the table to light it. He does not return her gaze.

"Thank you."

"My pleasure."

He sits back down again and picks up the small book he had been reading. She relaxes. The cigarette was merely offered out of politeness, a gesture towards another lone individual. It is not a nudge or an invitation. Driven by this man's very aloofness Grace wants to pull him in.

"What are you reading?"

"Oh, just this." He flashes the cover of the compact, slender book towards her. She can't see the name of the book or the author but picks up fleetingly a sketch of a man's face and a woman's face – both separate, melancholy.

"Oh," she answers, stupidly stumped for anything else to say.

He returns his attention to the book, turning the pages slowly. He seems to want to suck up the words off the page in the same way he draws the smoke into his lungs – fiercely, avidly. She becomes more and more curious about this slim volume and, in contrast to her earlier feelings, hopes that Guy will delay his arrival, so that she might take down the book from the shelf once he had finished with it.

Meanwhile, she sits immobile, not wishing to offer him any distraction. It is rare enough, in this masculine country of wild game, baking heat, roaring aero engines, to see anyone read anything other than weather reports, news digests, departmental memos. He is tall. Like most of the flying station crew, he is still boyishly thin, despite the excellent rations. The bony joints in his exposed knees, wrists, fingers rub against the underside of his skin. He finishes his cigarette long before she finishes hers, adding the filter to the pile of stubs in the bronze pressed ash tray in front of him.

She lets the smoke wreathe into the air from her own cigarette and watches while he runs a rounded thumb nail along the sharp lower edge of his moustache or under the cuff of his long ribbed socks.

She knows the protocol in this far-flung outpost, to speak to anyone who finds themselves alone. At drinks parties, sports days, funder raisers, everyone has to be scraped into the middle of the pile. It isn't quite the done thing to take a step back, to simply be an observer to the bonhomie, the camaraderie. The guffaws and back-slapping suit Guy better, his restlessness matched by the criss-crossing of shouted greetings, invitations issued and accepted, wagers honoured.

So it is that Grace finds herself simultaneously becalmed by this unusual juxtaposition of herself and this silent man and yet, disturbingly, exhilarated.

When Guy comes to collect her, it is clear that there had been no procurement meeting. Another convenient lie with which to wipe his face clean.

The two men nod to each other. "Who's that?" Guy asks as, gripping her arm tight, he steers her through the car park. Has he forgotten his promise to buy her dinner?

"No idea."

That night, he wants her to sit with him as he lies in a cool bath. "Take your blouse off. Let me look at you." She sits on the lavatory seat, leaning uncomfortably against the down pipe. The peeling rust and paint scratch her bare back.

Against the constant drip drip drip of the cistern, Guy is telling one of his long-winded stories that neatly and disingenuously puts him in the right and mocks the complete lack of sense of his colleagues. A rim of soap scum wavers between the cooling water's edge and the bath's enamel.

Moonlight reaches through the quiet night to smear itself on the dimpled bathroom window. She thinks of her children, her home town, so far away. Her heart aches. Nigel seems to be making a good fist of things now in Wellington but who's to know what his life is really like? Letters arrive now and again but she's sure a lot more is unsaid than said. Just how is he in his New World?

And Seb, shortly to leave Portsmouth and take up at Wandsworth College. She had wanted to keep Seb closer to her for longer; it had seemed important for them both. But sending him to school in England was not her decision. Only for Sorcha being beyond the bounds of Guy's ambition had she been allowed to keep the girl at home. Except that now, in an arrangement to forgo the unpaid bills, Sorcha is part weekly boarder, part assistant at the Bulawayo Road Colonial School. Approaching forty years old and Grace's life seems all but done.

"Push your breasts together." Her skin is cooling, her nipples erect. She kicks off her shoes and hooks one leg over the bath tub. Her toes tease the water.

He tugs roughly at his foreskin, his floating penis greying in the lowering light. Doesn't that hurt, she wonders? His eyes graze her flattened, exposed white thighs, boring into the dark place. She could, if she let herself, feel the first stirrings of arousal. But she won't allow herself tonight.

Guy grunts at his recalcitrant penis. "Do that thing that you do." He wants her to dance for him. To strip and expose herself completely. To force his attention. To virtually dismember herself and stick herself to him.

"No, not tonight, darling." To gainsay him is a gamble. But she is tired. She hasn't eaten since lunchtime. She's cold. And she's old. "I can feel a headache coming."

"Oh, very well. Don't say I didn't offer."

Grace laughs to flatter him. "Oh, I would never say that, darling. You are a good husband."

He grunts and swears as, levering himself upwards, his heels slide from beneath him. He splashes back in the bath, twisting so he's facing the dripping wall. His legs are bent apart, awkward and ungainly, two red pressure marks on his buttocks. She looks away quickly and picks up a towel.

Guy stands like a child in the emptying bath, allowing Grace to rub him down. She wraps him tightly. "Off you go now. Bedtime." She knows he likes to be nannied. "I'll just have one more cigarette then I'll come and join you."

She cleans the bath and walks through to the sitting room. There is a delicious freedom to her solitude, to her uncovered breasts. Stretched out in the chair, the moon seems a different creature to the one looking in on her and Guy through the bathroom window. More like a wistful lover, too far away to catch her except in its light, yet close enough to know her thoughts. She smokes her cigarette slowly, in no rush to go to bed.

What of the airman who, earlier that evening, had offered her a cigarette? Young. Probably closer to Nigel or Seb's age than hers. Dark hair, glossy like a blackbird's feathers. Lean but strong. He had glanced at her briefly, she knows, more out of inattentive politeness than curiosity. But hadn't he then looked up from his book when he thought she wasn't looking? Taken her in with his warm, brown eyes? Hadn't he then seemed more restless, distracted by her presence? For a brief moment she imagines sitting, semi-naked amongst the rough hurly burly of the other drinkers in the bar, waiting for the unknown airman to glance up from his book.

She must go to bed. With any luck, having been exercised rudely by whichever particular office assistant it was and taken an early bath, Guy won't be troubling her tonight.

Chapter 5

May 1952

Grace
Belvedere Park
Salisbury, Rhodesia

A letter from Kitty! She will be coming up to Salisbury for a few days to collect supplies for the farm and wouldn't it be a gas if they could meet up. Let's meet at the Ad Astra club, she suggests as it would give them a chance to ogle the new flying school recruits. Grace memorises the details of their meeting and scrumples up the letter. She would pick the right time and place to mention this to Guy.

The servant keeps his back to Grace as she levers off the hotplate, exposing cold, grey ash inside the range. The fire would be lit in time for the evening meal, despite there being a perfectly serviceable electric oven, swallowing up Kitty's lewd suggestions. She mutters, 'Thank you', as she leaves the kitchen, although thanks for what? For not turning his accusing eyes on her? For still turning up for work after Guy had beaten his brother's face to a pulp? She can never recall the man's name and has to stop herself from calling him Jacob. The sound of chopping crescendos as she pulls the door to behind her and steps out into the cool corridor.

*

"Darling! How lovely to see you!" Kitty calls across the bar lounge, over the still empty tables and chairs.

Grace steps tentatively into her embrace. Despite her rough existence on the remote farmstead and the distance into town, she always manages to look immaculate. Grace envies Kitty's tightly cinched waistline and button through pencil skirt. "What are you having to drink?" There is a large drink on the table between them. Kitty's heel topples. It is probably not her first of the day.

Kitty lights a cigarette, signals to the barman and chatters about the two-hour journey through the bush from their farmstead, Collinson's Ridge. "Listen to me! Haven't spoken to anyone half normal in ages." It is a different life for Kitty, and Grace wonders if she could have coped any better with life beyond the city. "It just seems when things go wrong, they go wrong on a monumental scale." Would Grace have the wherewithal to cope with crop failure, drought, lions? Would Guy have been a different man if he had realised his dream of becoming a farmer? "Are you any closer to moving out? To buying a farm?" Kitty asks. Grace shakes her head.

"No. It seems Guy's just too indispensable to the Ministry for them to let him go. He's tried, you know. Several times. But they keep giving him more work to do, telling him that he's the perfect man for the job, no one can quite handle the figures like he can. You know the sort of thing."

Kitty's wan smile shows she believes this little fiction no more than Grace does. "Well, it's probably a wise choice. Life's terribly, *terribly* hard you know." Another little fiction that Grace, in turn, overlooks.

"Will you excuse me for a minute, Kitty?"

"You going to the lav? I'll come with you."

"No, it's alright. You go. I'll mind our drinks."

Kitty gives her a queer look but doesn't argue, rising heavily. "Barman! Two more gin rickeys please," before tottering off, swallowed by the swing doors.

In her absence, Grace moves to the dark corner. Kneeling on the seats, she scans the books for one that matches the small volume the young airman was reading.

"What you doing there?" Kitty comes clattering along the lino flooring and pulls Grace off the banquette. "Come on. Quick sherbert before we go shopping. You alright? You're looking a bit off?"

Grace nods her head brightly and grips Kitty's arm as they high-step back to their table.

Kitty's chauffeur takes them the short distance from the aerodrome into town. They drive slowly through the heavy heat past the stone steps and porticoed entrance of the Post Office. Open-air vendors shout into the car. None of it makes sense. Her ears are buzzing and her heart is pounding. What are they doing here? The formal parks, the government buildings, the street lamps create a strange illusion of being back in a gentler, more temperate England. Oh, that she were back home. This place is not her place. She's not one of Kitty and Clive's sort, plundering the land. How much longer does she have to stand by and watch Guy's ambitions slip further and further away? Why are her children on three different continents?

"Kitty! Kitty! Stop the car. I need to get out!"

"What's the matter, pet?"

"I don't feel well. I need some air."

Kitty taps on the driver's seat and he pulls over onto the wide pavement. Grace glimpses the ornate park gates, the carefully raked gravel walkways within, the verdigris lion's head fountain, extravagant floral tubs. "Don't worry about me. I'll be fine. I just need…I just need…I don't know…air."

"Shall I come with you?"

"No!" Grace leans in through Kitty's window and concentrates on speaking calmly. "I'll see you in Dobey's Department Store in an hour."

Kitty's driver moves on and she turns into the park. How very English it all seems with its pollarded limes lining the long, straight avenue, Busy Lizzies jam-packed into the verges, the hiss of water hoses. Yet how unlike England in its heat, its smell, its deep blue, cloudless sky. Very possibly the only way home is if Guy's world collapses. If he is denied his ambition. Which would be the most intolerable? Staying here or going home, Guy broken?

"Mind your step!" She is aware of someone in the blue serge of a flying uniform appearing suddenly at her side.

"Sorry," she blusters, feeling herself brusquely pulled to one side. A young boy on a bicycle is careering towards her, his face wet with tears, mouth pulled open in panic. The bicycle skitters and bounces on the loose stones, clearly beyond the control of its rider. "Marcus! Marcus!" calls the boy's Nanny, running while pushing a large pram.

"I've got him," the man calls out, as he scoops the boy under the arms and clear of the bike, which topples and slides a few yards, coming to rest at the top of a long flight of steep stone steps.

Grace feels a sharp pain in her ankle from being thrown off course. The boy is wailing, thrashing out at both his Nanny and his rescuer, "You bloody idiot. What did you do that for? I was alright."

"Marcus! That is no way to speak to this nice gentleman. You would have hurt yourself if he hadn't stopped you. Now, say sorry for being so rude."

Apologies are evidently beyond the boy, defiantly holding onto his belief that he would have come to no harm at all, that it was down to the unwanted and unwarranted interference of this stranger, two strangers, that his bike is now beyond use. This is how it starts, Grace thinks. This unshakeable sense of self, this absolute sense of rightfulness, within the small frame of a four-year-old which will take root and grow and grow. A son of the Empire.

"Well, I think you are a very rude young man," Nanny tuts, looking to her charge's rescuer for confirmation. The boy shrugs.

Grace feels she should occupy herself in some way so, rather than seek to comfort the unappealing boy, she grips the handle of the pram and gently rocks the sleeping baby.

"I'll see what I can do about the bike," the man says, glancing at Grace as if having forgotten she was there. He glances back at her a second time and smiles. "I think it's a simple matter of putting the chain back on."

"I'd be so grateful. I mean, we would *both* be very grateful, wouldn't we Marcus?" Nanny says.

Lifting the bike off the ground and spinning the pedals, he manages to right the chain. "A bit scratched, and you'll need to hammer out the mud guard a bit. But no real harm done."

The boy makes slow work of returning to his bike, while Grace continues to jiggle the pram. "If everything is alright, I'll go then," Grace offers to the inattentive group. Walking tentatively, her ankle clicking with each step, she moves off down the path towards the centre of the park.

What a curious little episode that had been.

"Wait! I say! Miss!" Grace turns at the shout. Running towards her is the boy's rescuer. He arrives at her side, slightly out of breath. "Sorry. Shouldn't shout, I suppose. Had to reunite the young lad with his bike and plump up his feathers a bit. Think his pride took a bit of a knock."

Grace smiles. "I know what you mean. He didn't look too pleased. Not sure that the Nanny has him under firm control."

"It's more the other way round, if you ask me. Think the little lad has Nanny firmly in his sights."

There is a pause in the conversation; neither seeming to know what to say next. Grace studies the airman, the side of his face, as he gazes off into the mahonia bushes. Why had he stopped her?

"Lovely day…"

"No real harm done…" They both speak at once and then laugh awkwardly. Loudly.

"I just thought I should check you were alright. I hope I didn't startle you too much with that barrel-roll manoeuvre."

"No, no. I'm grateful. You saved the boy from certain harm and me from being knocked down. I wonder how he will tell the tale, once he's recovered his composure."

"Joint mission. Both crates safely returned to base. That sort of nonsense."

They both turn to continue walking. "You must be stationed at the base."

"Yes. Number Five Flight Training School. Based at RAF Thornhill. Teaching navigation, night flying, that sort of thing. One of those relics from the war. Never quite made it home. What about you?"

"My husband works at HQ in the Supply Department. We've been here since '47, five years now, nearly. Our plan had been to go into tobacco." Grace stops herself. Guy would call it prattling. Telling strangers what they had no business knowing.

"Yes?"

"Oh, well, you know how it goes."

"Yes. Of course." He extends his hand. "Patrick, by the way."

"Grace."

"Well, Grace, if you are sure you are alright, I'll be on my way."

"Perfectly fine. Thank you."

A squirrel runs ahead of their feet, skittering and checking back over its shoulder every few steps as if trying to keep them within its sight. As if leading them onto a destination of its choosing. Strange, she thought, why wouldn't such a wild creature scurry away, into hiding? It is fat and a little threadbare. It stops to gnaw at a bare patch on its inner thigh. Fleas.

She still feels the shock of the young child's near miss. A shock compounded by the homesickness that had previously assailed her in the car with Kitty.

She glances up into the nearest tree, a movement catching her eye. The squirrel. Two thoughts collide in her mind. Chasing squirrels through Sefton Park on her way home from school and an echo replaying in her mind. The sound of his voice. A hidden inflection. An unconscious elision of words. A faint, throaty explosion.

"Forgive me asking. But are you from Liverpool?" she asks.

"Well, once upon a time. Why? Are you?" Patrick looks puzzled. Guy had always been rather keen that she mask her Northern origins, encouraging Grace to model her accent and vocabulary on the BBC World Service they listened to each evening. Being from the Scottish Midlands, he'd felt that his own accent was immune from derision.

"Yes! Yes, I am! Or was! Grew up on the Wirral, went to school in New Brighton. My husband and I married in Port Sunlight where we lived before we came out here."

They turn and fall into a slow step together. It seems to Grace that they are about to step through a hidden door, into a magical, crystal palace, not unlike the Palm House in Sefton Park.

"I know New Brighton. Used to swim in the Lido there. With my sisters and my mother." His voice diminishes and his face dips into sadness. "I'm sorry." He shakes his head. "Memories."

The path through the close-clipped grass and rhododendrons stretches ahead of them. Beyond, the noise and bustle and fumes of the city and her appointment with Kitty at Dobey's department store.

"I think I've seen you at the Ad Astra Club, actually," she says.

He raises his head and glances quickly at her, showing no apparent recognition. And why would he? Each day was made of a thousand tiny collisions and crossings, all mostly leading to naught.

"Oh?"

She should hurry for it is nearly four o'clock and, although Kitty is rarely on time, Grace does not wish to be late. Nor does she wish to leave.

"Do you think you will go home?" she asks.

"Can't go home. Don't really know where home is."

Surely, she wants to say, home is where... But she checks herself. Maybe he too has no family left in that cold, rusting, dying seaport. He had mentioned a mother and a sister.

"Do you have any family?" The words come tinkling out of her mouth with the false cheer of a cocktail party. Inwardly, she fears the answer.

"No."

So that hadn't proved to be a very fruitful line of enquiry either.

She remembers watching him read at the Club within the small circle of light, drawn to his stillness. His good looks are no less diminished in the strong sunshine. A faint shadow collects below his cheekbones. Wide-set eyes balance a strong nose and mouth. He is tall, powerfully built. But possibly one of those indirect casualties of war.

"There's time yet," she offers. "We need to think to the future. Rebuild."

"Possibly. You're the only person I've met in a long time who knows the places back home. So many of the guys in my former squadrons were…well, we all know that line, 'Three of our aircraft failed to return'. Others have dispersed, goodness knows where. At least here, I'm spared too many reminders. Got a job to do, training air crews to be battle ready or for a future in civilian aviation. Whichever comes."

They walk in silence to the park gates. A sentry, sweltering in faux dress uniform, rolls the ornate iron work open for them. Grace stares at a small wheel bucking and jolting over the pebbles and rubble caught in the runnel. The whole contraption screeches and groans. They wait to pass between the gap, Patrick throwing a quick salute to the attendant before turning to Grace, hand extended.

"It has been nice to meet you…"

"Grace," she says quickly, in case he might have forgotten. "My name is Grace. Grace Lennox. *Mrs* Lennox."

"Patrick Frobisher."

"Patrick. I hope, truly, that you get home or find somewhere to call home. It is important."

"Well, maybe."

They part. Grace walks along Buckingham Street, the sun glinting and flashing from office windows and car mirrors, heat burnishing the soles of her shoes. After walking for twenty minutes, she arrives at the department store. Another lackey in a dress uniform opens the door and bows deeply. The coolness within soothes her. Long-armed fans stir the perfumed air, silk scarves flutter in the breeze. Another attendant operates the clanking cage elevator to the roof garden and tea rooms. No sign of Kitty. No surprise. She won't stay and have a cup of tea here, despite her dry throat, but will go home and ask Arnold (Arnold! That's his name) for one. That way, maybe, she could justify a taxi home.

Arnold answers the doorbell. The servant is agitated and looks worried.

"What's the matter? Are you unwell?" Grace asks.

"No, ma'am." He replies loudly, closing the door with a slam behind her, making her jump. "You are home now, ma'am."

"Indeed, I am," she replies, unwinding her headscarf. "Could you bring me some tea on the veranda, please. I'm parched."

"Certainly." Arnold holds out his hands for her scarf and handbag.

"Not to worry," Grace says. "I'll take these up to the bedroom myself."

"Please, ma'am. Allow me." He folds his hands emphatically over the straps of her bag, tugging it and her scarf towards him.

She is about to insist when a commotion on the upstairs landing catches her attention. Guy and Kitty laughing; his a rolling, booming laugh, hers a high-pitched whinny. It sounds for all the world as if Guy has just slapped Kitty on the rump. She stands at the bottom of the stairs, to meet them, eyes wide open.

"Darling! You're home!" Guy fixes his eyes on hers, as he comes down the stairs. Arnold squeezes past in the tight hallway on his way to the kitchen, whistling disapproval between his teeth.

Kitty, to her credit, only misses a tiny beat before calling out, "Needed to use your lavatory! Guy here kindly showed me the way."

Grace stands against the painted concrete wall to allow them both to pass.

Chapter 6

June 1953

Grace
Collinson's Ridge, Umtali
Manicaland Province, Rhodesia

"Come out to the farm. Sorcha must be at a loose end now school's finished," Kitty had written. "It will be good for both of you to get away, right away." Grace is not sure if, hidden within that remark, is the suggestion that it would be good for Grace – and possibly even Sorcha – to get away from Guy. The invitation does not seem to include Guy.

How much does Kitty know or guess about Guy? Unlikely that Guy would have told her about Jacob. It was all dealt with quietly and unofficially and expensively. But the couple of hundred miles between Salisbury, and Umtali and Kitty and Clive's farm – the news might have seeped along the dusty tracks through the veldt, like the first November rains on the parched and cracked earth. If only she could put the whole sorry business out of her mind.

And what of that other sordid business? That day a year ago when she came home and found Guy and Kitty on the top landing looking down at her over the bannisters, while Arnold grappled with her coat and bag.

Not only is her husband capable of pummelling a man till his cheekbones shatter, but he is an adulterer too. Kitty is not the first, by any means, but she is the closest. And in Grace's own home.

Kitty had breezed down the stairs, loud and effusive as usual. "Just been to powder my nose, darling." She had studied Kitty's nose, slightly reddened and glistening and definitely unpowdered. Her dried unpainted lips. Her tousled hair. Her eyes fell to Kitty's handbag on the hall table. Kitty's eyes fell to it too, before glancing ruefully at Grace. Kitty, the very model of chic, despite her rural life, would never make a trip to the bathroom to 'repair her face' without her handbag. A moment's flash passed between them during which Grace wearily handed over yet another triumph to her supposed friend, and Kitty summoned a silent apology for her lapse in manners and civility. The women shrugged and moved away from each other, blaming life in this fly-blown, hard-drinking, dream-dealing outpost.

Olivia returns her attention to the letter and Kitty's handwritten scrawl. "We get quite a few flight trainees and instructors staying in the chalets in the hot months, if they've got annual leave and don't want to go all the way home. Dutch, Canadian, British. Go on, Grace. She'll have a great time. I'll pay her some pocket money. It will keep her occupied for the next few months and, you never know, she might be able to bag herself a nice Flight Lieutenant."

Grace thinks it might on the whole be a good idea if Guy has no objections. "She'll be a sort of hostess. Obviously Kitty's got enough people to do the menial work. Sorcha can chat to the shy ones, make up a hand at bridge, that sort of thing. Kitty will take good care of her."

"Well, I don't want her spending all summer hanging around at swimming galas and quiz evenings. Let her go and find out about working life for a change."

So it was agreed that Grace and Sorcha would travel overland together when Sorcha finished school in a few days' time.

Grace wrote back. "Sorcha is very young for her age. She has not been exposed to much of life, other than moving out here. I am entrusting her to you, entrusting that you will keep her out of harm's way. Goodness knows, some of the behaviour at the base is rowdy enough. I wouldn't like to think Sorcha is being exposed to any nonsense while the men are on furlough. But Guy and I agree that it would be a wonderful experience for our daughter and we are very grateful to you and Clive."

Grace is quietly happy that plans are being made on Sorcha's behalf, for she herself is ill equipped to help her daughter with the next step of her life. How can she possibly help her daughter towards independence when she has none herself? Maybe it would be useful if she did meet someone eligible while at Kitty's.

"I feel you've barely been home," Grace says with a moue, watching Sorcha as she rushes around her bedroom packing her cases.

"Well, like Daddy says, I can't stay here all summer."

"While you're away, have a think about what you'd like to do. Afterwards. Provided you don't…"

"Don't what?"

"Nothing."

"What? Get eaten by lions or run off with a bushman?"

"No. Now you're being silly. No, I just think you need to decide if you want a…" Grace pauses while she thinks of a suitable word. "A…career."

"Oh. One of those."

"What are the other girls in your school doing? Anything that might interest you?"

"Dunno. Not much. Some are going to secretarial college, to learn typing and shorthand." Sorcha mimes a yawn. "Some are going back to England. Some are just going to hang around and do voluntary work and be decorative until someone snaps them up."

Sorcha looks around the utilitarian lodgings, obviously thinking it falls far short of the right milieu for her ambitions. How like your father you are, Grace thinks to herself. Both troubled by an unappeasable ambition and a sharpened sense of comparative inferiority. Both hard to place. "What do you think I should do?"

Grace laughs one of her short laughs. "Don't ask me, darling. Ask your father. He knows more about that sort of thing." Maybe Sorcha might even catch herself one of the new wave of buccaneers coming out to Africa. Those into precious metals or oil. "Anyway, darling, enough of this talk. Let's get you packed up."

Kitty's car comes for them at ten o'clock as arranged. Grace and Sorcha sit in the back of the Wolseley, baking. The driver is courteous but not inclined to say very much. "It's getting hotter," Grace offers to the back of his folded, glistening neck.

"Yes, ma'am."

"Phew," she addresses herself to Sorcha while fanning herself with a bergamot scented handkerchief.

Sorcha smirks. "Obviously."

They soon leave the city, its long, straight, orderly roads, cars parked chevron fashion in front of double storey, colonnaded shops, banks austere and prim and functional Anglican churches. At traffic lights, the driver shoos away opportunistic orange sellers. As the purple-flowering jacaranda trees, and magnolias give way to native baobab trees, Grace and Sorcha settle into their long journey. The road east is fast and straight, passing through dense forest and scrubland and cultivated mealie strips. Here and there they pass low storey adobe churches, neatly thatched, flamboyant biblical scenes painted on the outside walls.

Both Grace and Sorcha fall asleep. Grace wakes with a start, checking her watch. They have been travelling for two hours, another two hours to go. Are they where they should be? It is impossible to tell, little in the shrubby open landscape to place them. Isn't this an incredibly stupid thing they are doing, two females being driven off into the bush? How easily Kitty's driver could be intercepted, or even complicit in a plot to avenge Guy's savagery. She is unable to move, guilt and fear locking her limbs into paralysis, only her thin cotton dress flapping in the breeze from the driver's open window. Her eyes fix on the back of the driver's neck. He too is relatively immobile, the long straight road requiring only slight adjustments and manoeuvres from his hands. Perhaps she could speak to him, gauge by his response if he plans to abduct them or if his intention is simply to deliver them safely to Collinson's Ridge. The driver's eyes lock on to hers via the rear-view mirror. Her heart beats fast; her mouth way too dry to formulate any such question.

He reaches for something in the passenger footwell, swerving off the road as he does so. Sand billows past Sorcha's window, rat-tatting on the glass.

"With Mrs Simpkins's compliments," the driver mutters, correcting the car and handing backwards over his shoulder a tartan thermos flask.

"Thank you. Thank you very much." Grace stops her effusive thanks as Sorcha stirs and stretches. Seems we are not to be abducted and murdered, or worse, darling. Grace smiles broadly at her daughter who shuffles her knees and shoulder to the other side and goes back to sleep, unconcerned.

The coffee is black and bitter but has a welcome nip of something added to it. Trust Kitty, she thinks, gratefully.

Collinson's Ridge has changed quite considerably since their last visit. The house has grown lengthways and upwards, its earlier, humbler origins hidden beneath whitewashed plaster, black-as-tar wood framing and, incongruously, abundant wisteria. "I know, it looks like bloody suburban Surrey," Kitty says, noticing Grace's look. Grace rather likes it. Feels almost at home. The driver unloads their cases and drives round the back of the house. Should I tip him? Grace wonders, hoping that Guy or Clive would have dealt with such necessaries. "Come on in." Kitty walks up the steps bordered by a carved stone balustrade, across a flat lawn upon which a few men lounge, reading and smoking. The interior of the house is dark and cool.

They follow Kitty up the stairs to the guest rooms. Grace is a little surprised, and ungraciously gratified, to discover that the furniture and furnishings are becoming more and more sparse and shabby the further up into the house they go. "Here you are," Kitty says, opening a flimsy door into a low-ceilinged square room with two single beds and a marble washstand. "Moyo will bring your bags up shortly. Make yourself at home and come down when you're ready."

Grace and Sorcha stand in the centre of the bare floor, a smell like methylated spirits souring the air. There is little they can do until their bags arrive, so they appropriate a bed each, staring impassively out of the small window at farm workers pulling leafy groundnut plants out of the sandy red ground, scores of men and women working their way slowly up the regular shaped fields, shaking the soil free from the roots before exposing the husks to the sun to dry.

Sorcha looks challengingly at her mother.

"I'm sure our luggage will be here soon, darling," Grace says reassuringly, despite feeling they had been forgotten.

"This is sooo boring. Wish I had a cigarette."

Grace will not respond to her daughter's goading, so merely lifts her head slightly to gaze out of the window. Does she smoke? Where does she get the cigarettes from? Sorcha sighs loudly and flings herself backwards on her bed, clacking her loose sandals against the soles of her feet. Oh for goodness' sake, Grace wants to scream. Just stop it! I *know* we are marooned. I *know* we count for very little in anyone's estimation. Don't imagine for a minute that your father gives any more than the regulation two hoots about you, any more than he does about me. Otherwise, why are we here? The words spin round Grace's head as she lies immobile on the bed and the workers fan across the boundless field and the sun begins to sink towards the horizon.

Eventually, a servant knocks on their door with their luggage.

The next day Kitty shows them round the 'homestead', as she calls it. Behind the house is a low row of concrete dwellings under a mossy tin roof. Grace assumes these are servants' houses until Kitty explains that these are the paying guests' quarters. They look hot and uncomfortable, despite the shady verandah that runs the length of the building. Smoke rises from a point behind tall trees. "Don't go that way," Kitty warns Sorcha. "Out of bounds to us Westerners. Kitchen kaffirs only, ha ha."

"How many guests have you got staying at the moment?" Sorcha asks.

"Six. All from the flight training schools, a couple of them from Belvedere, your neck of the woods. You might know them."

They have to run almost to keep up with Kitty walking at a pace among storage silos and slab-sided barns and enormous riveted and braced water tanks. She turns and whispers conspiratorially, "Boring farts most of them. Ex-RAF, to a man. Heroes unto themselves. Spend most of their time reminiscing about the glory days of the war. Most of them don't have the guts or the funds to go back to the UK, so they find work at the airbases in Thornhill or Kumalo or Heany. The instructors are alright. Have to be, obviously. Need your wits about you to teach signals or navigation or armaments or flying, I appreciate that."

They stop outside a small hangar. "This keeps the sane ones occupied."

They peer into the gloom at a small aircraft. Standing around it, a handful of young men in overalls. The engine is coughing and spluttering, filling the space with pungent smoke.

"Well, relatively sane," Kitty qualifies before guiding them back towards the house. "We had one unfortunate type wander off into the bush once. Everyone thought, after they'd searched for him for days, that he'd been eaten by hyenas or gone loco. They found him after a fortnight or so. Ragged, burnt to a crisp, sobbing. Thought forty days in the wilderness would absolve him of his wartime sins. Wanted to go back for the remaining twenty-three. Miracle how he survived, really. The rest of them choose a more lingering death – drink themselves stupid, get 'scrubbed' and end up at the Salvation Army hostel in Salisbury until some friends club together for their passage home."

"Is this the best company to leave my daughter in?" Grace asks laughingly.

"Of course. They're all absolute darlings. Don't mind me. I just get a bit bored of the talk. If it's not the war, it's yields per hectare and leaf miners and termites. Sorcha is a lovely young woman. She'll have fun here."

It had been arranged that Guy would motor up on the Friday evening to bring Grace back to Salisbury, giving her two days at Collinson's Ridge to relax. Kitty is being extra-solicitous, as if she feels she owes Grace something. "If no one's about, just help yourself to drinks. The good stuff's at the back, behind the ice buckets. Don't stint yourself." Kitty squeezes Grace's elbow before shouting, 'Oy, you!' after a servant on the point of disappearing into the cool depths of the house. "God knows you deserve it."

For two days Grace watches her daughter mingle with a surprisingly natural effervescence, pouring drinks, moving garden furniture into the shade, cutting hair.

Grace sits on the lawn under a fringed cotton umbrella, its colours bleached by the sun. The air is hot and dry. Soon the autumn rains will come, cooling the air and calling an end to this sun-induced indolence. At this altitude, the air is clear and clean, spoiled only by the tang of aviation fuel when 'the crew' charge up the small Harvard's engine and take it for 'a jump'. The runway stretches behind the guests' quarters so that her first view of the plane after take-off is as it lifts noisily and precariously above the chimneys of Collinson's Ridge. From the lawn, she can clearly make out the features of the pilot and the co-pilot as they pull hard up into the air.

Sorcha comes out to ask if she would like a 'drink drink' seeing as it's now gone midday.

She wonders if she might take up painting.

Chapter 7

Late June 1953

Grace
Collinson's Ridge, Umtali
Manicaland Province, Rhodesia

Guy arrives after work on Friday night. Grace watches him drive up to the front door, leaving the car door open and the engine running before mounting the steps to the front door. Someone will garage it for him. He will expect it to be returned tomorrow with the dust of his journey removed, the water bottles filled, windscreen washed. He has too easily acquired a sense of what is his due and a self-righteous indignation if the small courtesies are not forthcoming.

How different he is to the young man from the Scottish Midlands she met on the Liverpool waterfront twenty-five years ago. Then she had felt a strange compunction to rub the back of his hands as if to warm him, to loosen some of his reserve, to see him laugh. That no longer seems quite so appropriate. Maybe she is the one who has changed the most.

She knows him well enough to see the little stabs of jealousy behind his eyes as he takes in the trappings of Clive and Kitty's success. Through hard work, luck and privilege they have created something remarkable. They stand in territory of their own making, five hundred acres of wheat and tobacco and groundnuts. What does Guy have to show for his endeavours in this foreign country? No chance now of going into farming on the wages of a provincial clerk.

Moyo stands by the door to receive Guy and his belongings. "Mrs Simpkins asked me to show you to the lounge and to be of service to you, Sir." Guy will be disappointed that Kitty and Clive themselves are not here to greet him. Wearily, she rises from her armchair to welcome him.

"Darling. You made it!" Her tone is false, affected.

"Of course I made it," Guy returns grumpily. "What do you expect? Ambush? Abduction?" Grace laughs before he can accuse her of being silly and steers her husband towards the sideboard.

"Whisky?"

"Wouldn't mind. Where is everybody?"

"Clive had to go into Umtali on business and Kitty's getting ready for dinner, I believe."

"Oh. And Sorcha?"

"She's helping in the kitchens." A look of distaste crosses his face. "Well, you know, finishing touches, that sort of thing." Guy nods and looks round the room at the paintings, the ormolu clock and burnished pier glasses. "Bit grand in here, isn't it?"

"Shush, darling, someone will hear you."

"Mmmm. Anyway, how are you?" He bends to kiss her cheek. His lips are wet and cold. She represses a shiver.

"Fine."

"Good."

Guy sits heavily in a wicker chair, almost instantly holding out his glass for a refill. She is glad of something to do for it looks as if the conversation has run its course.

*

They are eight for dinner. Kitty and Clive, Grace and Guy, Sorcha, two flying school instructors – Giles and Hugo – plus a fidgety young man called Alex. The Brown Windsor soup, despite the heat, is delicious. Sorcha proudly brings out her entremets of Pea Mousse served in glass moulds. Only Alex eats his with delicacy and appreciation, the other men barely noticing what has been put in front of them. Guy is well soused by the time the goat curry arrives. Grace feels almost ecstatic at the aroma and spices. Is it possible to get drunk on food, she wonders, as her head swims and her eyes water? A small mound of barely frozen apple sorbet leaves her restored and in impatient anticipation of Sorcha's Chestnut Meringue.

"Delicious, darling," she whispers to her daughter, leaning round the back of an airman. Sorcha blushes proudly. Grace is pleased that Sorcha shows a talent for cuisine – a talent that could prove useful in the future if she were to marry well.

"Thanks, Mummy."

"Yes. Full marks to our budding chef here," bellows Clive.

A babble ensues round the table as the company variously raise their glasses and toast Sorcha. The last voice is Guy's. "It seems good things come from tins after all." The noisy appreciation subsides. "Shut up, you oaf," Kitty mutters under her breath. Alex looks between mother and daughter. He offers a rueful smile in consolation.

"Have you heard the rumour that the training bases are likely to be mothballed in a year or so?" asks Giles. Or possibly Hugo. Guy looks up tetchily.

"Oh! Why's that?" Kitty asks.

"Well, everyone expects the Koreans to stop fighting themselves in a month or two. No need to train up recruits to fly with the American and Australian air forces against North Korea.

Besides, everyone's bankrupt and war weary. Government's pulling its horns in. Churchill wants a United States of Europe to stand up against the Soviets. Means we can step things down a little."

Guy's voice thunders over the scattered dining things. "A toast, methinks."

"Hear, hear."

"A toast to Her Majesty. Our most gracious sovereign."

"Who do you mean?" quips one of the airmen in a fake Cockney accent. "Her up London? Or our very own Queenie, Mrs Kitty…?"

"No, no," Guy insists. "It is only right and proper." He stands awkwardly, sending a wine glass clattering to the floor. "Ladies and gentlemen. Please be upstanding."

"Oh, for goodness' sake, sit down." Kitty pulls on Guy's sleeve. "Nobody toasts the Queen these days." Guy rocks on his heels, holding onto the back of his chair, his face growing redder and redder. "Really, it's Clive's job," Kitty whispers across the table to Grace.

A panic rises in Grace's breast. If she doesn't stand shoulder to shoulder with him, he risks becoming even more of a laughing stock than he already is.

She pushes her chair back to stand. Alex stands too. One by one, they all rise to their feet.

"Oh, very well. If you insist. Charge your glasses, everyone." Clive calls a servant over and Port appears in the middle of the table, together with tiny stem glasses. "Fill up. Fill up."

Guy stands firm, beads of sweat forming on his forehead. There is a smear of green in his moustache; a brown streak runs down his white shirt. He refuses the offer of Port, calling instead for more whisky. Brusquely, he brushes away the ice tongs in the servant's hand. "Oh Guy, oh Guy," Grace whispers under her breath.

"Oh, well, *noblesse oblige*, I suppose," sighs Clive. "Thank you, Guy for reminding us to honour our new Queen. I'd like to offer the loyal toast. The Queen."

"The Queen."

"The Queen."

The table quietens once they sit down again, all liveliness gone. "Shall I tell a joke?" asks one of the airmen. He pauses during the general murmur of assent. "Right. There is an Englishman, a Frenchman and an Italian. They are wandering the bush when they get captured. Before the chief puts them in boiling water they are all offered one wish."

Guy finishes manoeuvring himself back into his seat. He looks bored, disinterested. "Come on, Guy," Grace wants to say. "Buck up."

"So, the Frenchman asks for wine. 'Bring mon ami a glass of wine', the chief demands. To the Italian, he repeats the question, 'What is your dying wish?'. The Italian asks for a beautiful woman. 'Bring my youngest daughter', replies the chief…"

The airman pauses for effect.

Guy runs a pair of grape scissors between his fingers.

"Then, when it is the Englishman's turn, he says he wants the chief's strongest warrior to punch him in the guts. The chief agrees to this strange request and calls over his youngest son, who deals him a hefty blow to the belly. In a flash, the Englishman pulls out a submachine gun from his boots and kills all the Africans around."

"Ha, ha, ha, ha, ha."

"Shut up, Guy, that's not the end of the joke."

"Yes, it is," replies Guy. "Because the Frenchie and the Itie then both turn to our man and say, 'Why didn't you do that in the first place?' We've all heard it."

Sorcha looks puzzled. "Why didn't he do it in the first place?"

"It's because the Englishman didn't want to look like the primary aggressor, so he manipulates events to make it look as if the death and carnage are not his fault but the inevitable and necessary outcome of the barbarism of the native." Alex addresses his words to Sorcha while holding Guy in his sights, as if his measured tone might calm him down.

"Is that funny, Mummy?" Sorcha asks Grace behind her hand. Grace waggles her head, non-committally. Oh, my goodness, this is all going so horribly wrong.

"Maybe Guy wishes to freshen up," Kitty interjects. "Moyo, would you be so kind as to escort Mr Lennox to his room."

"Don't worry. I can take a fucking hint," Guy roars, flapping the servant's proffered arm away.

"Guy!" Grace feels her patience on the verge of finally snapping.

"Fuck off, yourself."

"Oh, I am really so sorry. I don't understand what's got into my husband. I'll go and attend to him."

"Sit yourself down, Grace," orders Kitty. "You will do no such thing. He's had a few sherberts too many. Not a problem. A man's prerogative when he's on leave. He'll be fine in the morning. You stay down here and enjoy yourself."

Grace nods, her head low, her hands in her lap. Sorcha's hand creeps into hers. She squeezes it tight for just a small moment.

This is a night when her husband will rage most protestingly against the incompetence of his wife, the weakness of his daughter, the death of Empire and all his dreams. All his power, all his worth, all his drive will devolve to his penis.

Grace sits at the dressing table, making herself ready for the night ahead. He has obviously been waiting for her in the half interval between his ignominious dismissal from the dinner table and when she felt she could reasonably leave her hosts.

She fixes her hair so that her neck is exposed and sits mutely, hands in her lap. A warm mannequin.

He is working away vigorously at his erection, grunting rhythmically. One night he went too far and discharged himself on the floor. It glistened on the rug. "Less than you could put in your eye," as Kitty might say. The thought of her friend's derision makes her smile.

Occasionally, just occasionally, an accidental climax will come her way. She can never abandon herself to its sinuous, winding pleasure or sing out her full-throated delight. All she can do is mutely swallow down its magic.

"On your knees!" She walks round to where Guy is standing, careful not to tread on his bare feet in her heels. She kneels on the stool and places her hands firmly on the dressing table, strong, braced. Her breasts are free now. He pulls her panties down to her knees, his unhindered penis swaying. As he slides it beneath her, she wonders what it must be like to be born with one. Such easy pleasure. A willing playmate. Not a coy, slippery thing like her own sexuality.

Suddenly, like a fugitive, he slips inside her. His need is urgent tonight. Three hard thrusts and it is all over. He steps away. Leaving her, he makes his way to the bathroom. She clambers down off the dressing table, her wrists bent stiff, her passion unspent.

Chapter 8

Early November 1953

Grace
Collinson's Ridge, Umtali
Manicaland Province, Rhodesia

"She saw it all happen," Kitty tells her quietly. "She had been sitting on the lawn when she heard the plane take off. Said she'd been talking to Patrick that morning..."

"Wait. Wait!" A black fog fills Grace's skull; her heart feels drained of blood. Kitty stops talking and looks questioningly at Grace. "Did you say, *Patrick*?"

"Yes. Why do you know him?"

"Flight Training School, RAF Thornhill?"

"Yes. Probably. Young man. Tall, dark, not much to say for himself."

Grace needs to sit down before her knees buckle. It could be no other. How could this have happened? She had told Patrick about Kitty and Collinson's Ridge. Did he have any expectation of meeting her out here? It would be absurd to think so.

Kitty is talking. "Are you alright? You're looking frightfully peaky. It has been a shock for everyone." Grace is not listening but closes her eyes and sees Patrick walking beside her, the utter sadness in his voice as he spoke of his family killed in the '41 Blitz.

The roughness of his uniform beneath her comforting touch. A squirrel. His quiet request that they meet again.

"Anyway, poor Sorcha. She pretty well saw everything."

"I'll go to her."

"Not just yet. I gave her some of my knockout drops. She's fast asleep. I'd leave her be. Sleep'll do her good."

"Thank you for taking care of her."

"Oh, she'll be alright. Young ones are resilient. It's not as if they were involved or anything." Grace looks sharply at Kitty. "No. Nothing like that. They got on quite well, spent a bit of time together. Poor girl. No wonder she's so upset. You get out of the way of this sort of thing, now the war's over. Clive's a bit cut up about the plane, mind you." Kitty chatters away as they climb the stairs to the first floor. "Do you want to see his room?"

"Patrick's?"

"Yes."

"Are we allowed? I mean, haven't the police made it out of bounds?"

"No. They came over yesterday, had a perfunctory look through his things and then left. Don't think they took anything. There were no diaries or 'notes', if you get my meaning. There was a half-finished letter to his mother, which is all a bit tragic in the circumstances. I suppose somebody will have to send it on. Come in."

Grace is drawn in to his room. "I thought most of your guests slept out back."

"He paid extra."

"Oh, I see."

Grace looks round the small, tidy room. "Do you think he meant to…you know…?"

"Lord knows," Kitty retorts, picking up and turning over

a pair of binoculars. "Bloody selfish, if he did. I mean, everyone's leaving. What are we supposed to do? I know it's coming to the end of the season, but even so. Do you want to read that letter?"

"No," Grace shakes her head vehemently.

"Suit yourself. Where *is* Fazakerly, anyway?" Grace watches as Kitty neatly folds the two pages of Patrick's unfinished letter in half and then in half again, wondering if his last communication would ever reach his mother. "I always think shoes are the worst." Kitty nudges a pair of black dress shoes with her toe. "There's very little else that's so personal. Our connection with the ground. Did you know some people cut up the shoes of the deceased, believing it's wrong to reuse them because, if you do, the soul will find no rest?"

"No, I didn't know that."

"Well, it's giving me the creeps in here. Come down when you and Sorcha are ready and we'll have a stiffener before you hit the road."

Grace nods silently, as Kitty leaves. She feels calmed being in his room. A faint smell of sandalwood and pine hangs around the wash basin. A damp towel lies scrunched next to the bowl. She picks it up and holds it to her nose, breathing in a complexity of masculine smells. A white toothbrush leans against the inner rim of a drinking glass. The room is neat and orderly, here and there a few objects out of place – a tie looped round a bed post, a packet of cigarettes and a lighter tossed hastily onto the eiderdown, laundry waiting to be collected. "Oh Patrick," she whispers. "Why?"

On the bed stand is the book Patrick had been reading at the Ad Astra Club. Deftly, she slides it into her handbag and leaves before sadness overtakes her and grief incapacitates her.

Grace tiptoes to the top floor and gently pushes open the door to the bedroom she and Sorcha shared a couple of months earlier. Sorcha is sitting on her bed, a cushion pulled into her belly.

"Darling child." Sorcha turns to look at Grace. Her face is gaunt and blotchy. She gulps air as if finding it impossible to speak, her airways impeded. "It's alright. It's alright. Hush now." Grace pulls her daughter's ragged head to her chest and rocks and soothes her.

"It was just awful. Awful. He'd been fine in the morning. We'd been chatting about Liverpool. He knew it was where you were from…"

"I know. Don't talk now."

"I just heard this almighty roar and looked up and it was like the plane was rocketing up into the sky."

"There, there. You're safe. It's all alright."

"And it just went ever so quiet and…and…"

"Sssh. Ssssh." Grace rocks her daughter harder and harder, a rag doll in her arms.

"And then everyone started screaming and then there was a massive ball of fire in the air."

Grace stops rocking and grips Sorcha by the shoulders, looking straight into her red veined eyes. If she is to be strong, then Sorcha must be strong. "Now listen to me, darling. Listen! You are upsetting yourself. This is not good for you. I know it has been a horrible episode but you must – *must* – put it out of your mind. Do you hear me?"

Sorcha snuffles and nods.

"The more you go over it in your mind, the more upsetting it will become. You must tell yourself that. Patrick is dead, for whatever reason. But life goes on. You are a young lady. You've got your whole life before you. Nobody is going to want to know you if you spend all your time snivelling. Are they?"

Sorcha shakes her head, blowing her nose loudly into a damp handkerchief.

"Good girl."

"Is Daddy here?"

"No, darling. He couldn't get away. He's busy at the base. But he sends all his love and says he can't wait to see you again."

"Mmm. Doubtful."

"Don't be like that. Now, remember what I said, and try to look a bit more cheerful. Time to pack up your things. I'm taking you home." Grace waits for the objection that doesn't come. "Put some powder and some lipstick on. Make yourself a bit more presentable. Understand?"

"Yes, Mummy."

"Good girl."

Waiting for Sorcha to come downstairs, Grace takes a seat behind a rattan screen. A large rubber plant hides her from view. She pulls the book from her bag. *The Lonely*. Both the title and author name, *Paul Gallico,* are written in italics across the cover. The man and the woman sketchily represented on the cover face inwards yet their dark eyes miss each other. They seem to float in an ominous sky, amongst dark clouds.

The pages are thick and fibrous, the colour of ageing distemper. She flicks through, noticing words and lines underlined in pencil with emphatic markings in the margins. Stars, arrows, scrawls – a maelstrom of pencil strokes.

A door closes noisily upstairs. She pulls a magazine onto her lap, to obscure the book. She should put it straight back where she found it, but that would entail returning to his quarters, which is unthinkable.

He is reading to her, his voice slow, chiming with the loneliness of all the boys called upon to do the impossible, to defend and uphold such bright truths within the muck and squalor of war.

They are the children of the sky, the wanderers who cannot find their way home.

She can hear the faint whininess of his accent, an amalgam of bog Irish and King Cotton, the accent of her home…

The loneliness of those who came too close to Heaven and Hell…

…and she wants more than anything to be able to cry.

How strange that he should find his way to Collinson's Ridge. And how utterly dreadful that the young man now lying cindered and charred in the morgue in Umtali is the man whose loneliness and homelessness she unwittingly exposed in the Belvedere Park in town.

Chapter 9

Late November 1953

Grace
Salisbury, Rhodesia

"I hadn't wanted to raise the matter with you before, while there was some degree of uncertainty." Guy is sitting opposite her, the light from the lowering sun shining through the veranda windows, enlivening the smoke from his cigar. She waits, hands in her lap, for him to continue. It must be an important announcement. She just wishes he would hurry up as Arnold is hovering, wanting to serve up the dinner. Arnold and their liver and bacon will have to wait. She shoots the servant a look that tells him to go back into the kitchen.

"Sounds intriguing, darling."

"Yes, well, as you may or may not know, some fairly significant changes are afoot. Only a few of us are privy to the truth of the matter, the rest of it is just hearsay and speculation." Oh, for goodness' sake, Guy, she wants to say. Everyone knows the base is closing. It's just a matter of when.

"Well, I *had* heard…"

"Well, don't believe everything you hear."

"No, of course not, darling."

Guy puffs on his cigar. It is probably a cheap one because the end burns quickly and drops ash onto his lap. His supply from the officers' mess must be dwindling, along with other perks of being affiliated to the Royal Air Force overseas.

"The upshot of it is…" Guy pauses for effect. "A few of us are being sent ahead. To prepare the way. That sort of thing."

"So, we are leaving?"

"In a nutshell, yes."

"Right-oh." This is not news to Grace, having already heard it from various sources around the place. Guy is being pensioned off, given gardening leave, because with no base to supply, who needs procurement wallahs? "When do we leave?"

"No final date has been given, but probably within a month or two."

"Where will we go?"

"Well, home, of course."

"Is this an official posting?"

"No. No. Time to move on I think. New horizons and all that." She glances at Guy blowing smoke up to the ceiling, his cheeks veiny and hyperextended. She might feel sorry for him. If only he were more *honest* about losing his job. Really, she wants to bash the pompous old prig over the head but it would be better to make little acknowledgement of the current situation and carry on regardless. Passing Guy on her way out to the kitchen, she pats him gently on his shoulder.

When it comes, the notice to leave is swift and matter of fact. They are required to vacate their accommodation within two months. Passage home via troop ship is provided and they are to present themselves at the ticket office in Bulawayo on 28 January.

She doesn't blame Guy for the complete reversal in their

affairs. How could she? It isn't his fault that, yet again, they are to join the migration of people streaming across the face of the globe. How the big events in the world shake down to affect hapless individuals. Nigel is probably the safest of them all in New Zealand. Seb seems to be doing alright at College. Some of the aircrew will undoubtedly stay in Rhodesia. There is talk of political instability but land is key. Kitty and Clive will be alright, owning land and having a few shekels in the bank.

Home! The thought of it sends a shiver of excitement zigzagging through Grace's whole body. It might pep Sorcha up a bit. Since Patrick's death, the poor girl has had no spirit.

"What's wrong with the girl?" Guy had wanted to know. "Can't you have a word with her? This is nonsense the way she is moping about, crying at the drop of a hat."

"I'll have a word with her."

Grace and Sorcha spend their afternoons packing belongings into crates to be sent ahead. "Is it true Daddy's got a job?" Sorcha asks, sitting in Guy's chair, screwing and unscrewing the wing nuts on a racquet press.

"Yes. With the Board of Trade in Liverpool."

"What will I do?"

"I am sure there will be lots of options for someone with your abilities."

"Like what?"

"Oh, I don't know. You've had a good education…"

"I can make a raised pork pie and embroider pretty napkins. Not sure how much call there is for that in this 'modern' world."

"We'll be alright. You'll be alright. Daddy will see to it."

Chapter 10

January 1954

Grace
Mozambique to Southampton

The ship, a British India vessel, stands tall, forward-looking, beside the teeming quayside at Beira, a brilliant, dazzling white against the blue sky. Sorcha marches mechanically up the gangplank, impervious to the bustle all around, troops returning from a day and a night's recreation mingling with the ship's staff, stevedores, hawkers.

"This way please, sir." A white-gloved steward directs them to their cabins in the centre of the ship. The corridors are tight, an unpleasant smell intensifying as the temperature grows warmer and warmer. Their accommodation is second class, rudimentary, windowless. Their steward introduces himself as Mohamed and bows a few degrees. Grace wonders if the small courtesies on board ship are graded, such that they are accorded a "Deck 8" sort of a bow. Not that it matters greatly – only to Guy who is fussing with the connecting door, ignoring Mohamed's patient wait for a tip.

Grace reaches into her purse for a shilling. "You shouldn't have done that," Guy whispers furiously. "It will only encourage him."

"I thought that was precisely the idea."

The ship has a peculiar, patched together orderliness to it, the several hundred troops outnumbering the paying passengers. Within two weeks they will all be home. She wonders, looking into passing faces, if everyone else shares the same depth of disappointment and fatigue and fear that are her own travel companions.

They are bringing little back with them. Theirs is only one departure among so many now that the stations and bases and outposts are closing one-by-one. Kitty had given them an elaborate carving of an antelope's head which Grace had stuffed in the bottom of a packing case. If it breaks, it breaks.

Despite the near nervous collapse of his daughter, Guy seems curiously buoyant at the prospect of their return to Liverpool – what he calls 'the Empire's second city'.

As for Sorcha, hopefully she will stand a better chance on home ground. "At least we'll be nearer Seb. You'd like that, won't you?" Grace had offered.

"Yes. That would be nice."

Grace hasn't yet told Sorcha of her father's plan to send her up to Scotland, to work in a cousin's hotel. That will need careful timing. But they are winning with Sorcha. She seems to be coming round again, regaining some of her bloom. After all, she isn't the only girl in the world to have come a near miss, to have taken a knock.

Yet, how many young men, like Patrick, would not be making it home? As the troops exercise and rest on the bow deck, Grace imagines, moving among them, the pale, insubstantial ghosts of the boys and young men who had lost their lives in Malaya, Korea, Singapore; younger brothers or cousins lost in the ten years since the end of the last world war.

Sorcha sits virtually immobile on the deck during the voyage home. Around her, the clear sharp screech of the drill sergeant's whistle, practice rifle shots, the troops' restlessness at variance with her stillness.

How different they are as a family to when they made the journey out eight years ago. Then, the children had spent hours running from side to side, counting and naming the dolphins that ran with them, cresting the wake of the ship, through the Red Sea and out into the Indian Ocean. She and Guy had stood together to watch the flatlands of Mozambique approach, the ship slowly navigating the waterways to its berth, hopeful of a new start. They looked forward to a fresh beginning as the children stamped on locusts jumping onto the ship's decks.

And now they steam the opposite way, passing north alongside the east coast of Africa, past Mombasa, gunfire ringing out in salute as they cross the Equator, Aden, the Tropic of Cancer, up the Red Sea. At Port Suez, they drop anchor out in the deeper water watching as nets of provisions – fresh fruit, vegetables, post – are hoisted from a supply ship. Would they see such luscious oranges, grapefruit, bananas back in England? Slow progress through the Suez Canal, the desert dotted with white buildings, tents strung beside green oases. The shipwrecks, victims of enemy bombing raids that she remembered at Port Said on the outward journey must have been cleared. The dhows gliding through the water as graceful as birds are unchanged.

As Guy dozes on deck, Grace withdraws Patrick's book from deep within her own suitcase. She opens the slim volume and reads quickly of the American airman, Jerry, based in Gedsborough Airbase, Lincolnshire. Is there any similarity between Jerry, Gallico's airman, and Patrick? The two of them subject to those great rolling destinies that strip a young man out of his familiar world and drop him into an alien and brutal place. Patrick – and Jerry – flying through the icy, choking air to drop death and destruction onto unknown civilians below. Could she imagine Seb or Nigel undertaking such a task?

Within the pages of the slim volume, Jerry travels through Scotland with his companion, Patches. Patches, a woman limited no less by her diminutive, make-and-mend sort of a name as her role as comforter and whisky-pourer to the morally challenged hero. Jerry's megrims – a wild, furious, drink-fuelled journey to oblivion in response to the horror of an airman's mission – are marked out in the text in a wild, furious hand. It can only be Patrick's hand. The pity of those young men, not natural destroyers, called upon to deal out such indiscriminate destruction. Doing the biding of others. Agents, ultimately, reciprocally, of their own doom.

Had Patrick simply come to the end of the line? What she had taken for quietness, stillness, acceptance, had that simply been a pause, a moment to think and reflect, before taking his own punishment? Had his sense of homelessness and loneliness unriven him from anything that might bring back hope and light and a future?

Sorcha's face floats above the ravaged text. Had she tried to provide, whilst at Collinson's Ridge, some of that feminine comfort and solace gentle Patches had offered to Jerry? Who knows? Or had Patrick hoped that Grace, herself, could have stilled his mind?

The ship sails on. After the Suez, they broach the Mediterranean, the Nile delta now all but a hazy, disconnected line on the horizon. Malta, Tunis. The captain announces that once past Algiers, they will lose sight of land for several days and passengers should prepare for rough weather in the Bay of Biscay.

Grace lends Sorcha a skirt and jumper of hers she had kept from the outward journey. They are musty, wrapped in tissue and oil cloth for all those years.

Finally, England. As they stand on the deck, watching the tall cranes form a guard of honour, she feels as if the mists of the Solent hide a gateway, that they are emerging from a different time, a different world, into cold, grey uncertainty.

And what will they make of their new life? Will Guy continue to hammer frenziedly against the anvil of his rage, sparks glowing in a fan all round him? Will Sorcha's white-cold heart be mettle enough for what lies ahead?

Sparrows hopped from girder to girder in the Customs shed while they wait to be processed and their luggage to arrive. In the foggy gloom, they board the boat train from Southampton to Waterloo.

Chapter 11

March 1954

Grace
Edmonton, London

Within a month of returning to England, a letter arrives from Seb informing them he is getting married and a date has been set. "July 24. All welcome. Suggest you might like to come down to London and meet the soon-to-be in-laws, the Whittakers."

The letter arrives mid-morning. Grace considers telephoning Guy at work but decides it will wait until he gets home.

Guy's reaction is one of disinterest. "Does he expect us to just drop everything and go and visit these people?"

"Well, yes. I expect so."

"Bloody marvellous. How do we know he's actually going to graduate with anything worthwhile? Why saddle yourself with a wife before you've even started out?"

"He has never been happier, apparently," she tells Guy, who shows no interest in reading his son's letter. "She's called Ronnie and she's on the same Technical Drawing course as Seb. She's already been offered a job in some sort of engineering capacity in Birmingham, so they will be moving there after the wedding. They have chosen to get married in the University chapel."

"Well, bully for them."

Guy's displeasure is irksome. Why can't he just be happy for the boy? She will have to approach the topic of meeting Seb's new family carefully at a later date.

"So, it's all sorted then."

"Would appear that way."

Alone in their rented kitchen she re-reads Seb's letter. "Dearest Mother and Father," he writes. Dearest? As if there might be others that are less dear. His writing tumbles and skitters across the flimsy blue paper. She scans down the page, endeavouring to extract meaning without the minute scrutiny needed to decipher each word. Much of the two-page letter tells them about Ronnie.

It is later agreed that Grace will represent the family and meet Seb's fiancé. She will offer Guy's apologies for the pressures of work not allowing him, on this occasion, to… She's become well versed in Guy's excuses and how to represent them as genuine.

Grace sees Seb straight away. He is sitting on a bench in the central concourse of the station, absorbed in his thoughts. His hair is longer and he twists a strand in his preoccupation.

"Seb! Seb!" she calls. He looks up, turning his head this way and that before pulling Grace tightly into him. His embrace is warm, strong, a man's embrace and she lingers for a tiny moment, breathing in his smell of carbolic soap and damp wool.

She taps him lightly – once, twice – on his chest with the flat of her hand and he releases her. That's enough, son.

They take a taxi from Euston and travel slowly out through to the suburbs. She wonders if she might ask the driver to close his window, for the air blowing into the vehicle is abrasively cold; the raised goose pimples on her arm part of a forgotten, even primitive, reflex after so many years of heat. But she's not sure it's polite to ask. Seb sits in the front and chatters to the driver who seems to be paying little attention. The driver is clearly not cold – his exposed forearm hangs out of the open window – so she distracts herself by watching the wind play in Seb's hair, fanning it into rosettes, until he might notice how cold she is getting and ask the driver to close the window.

Even the city is green. She'd forgotten the multiplicity of shades of green there are in England in her red and brown years in Africa. Each shade minutely different from the next. And grass. So much grass, growing over and around and up to the edges of things, like an animal's pelt. A line from school assembly comes to her mind. It truly is a pleasant land.

Pleasant, but broken. As the taxi speeds up, brick and concrete houses and shop fronts hurtle past the window. Every now and again, the light intensifies as they pass a no man's area of flattened rubble and debris. Colours are limited to the yellowed-out shop windows and deep purples of the buddleia growing in the wilderness. Much else is drab, uniform, un-showy.

Finally they arrive at Mr and Mrs Whittaker's house. Seb turns round in his seat, as if surprised to find his mother still in the back of the vehicle. She gives him a wan smile. It all feels very strange. Africa, clearly, is not home but nor is this humdrum, workaday street. She steps out onto the pavement, staring up at the peeling paintwork and cracked window panes of Roselea Villas. The low brick wall sends up little nubs of metal where, presumably, any wrought iron had been cut away and melted down for Spitfires. She hastily shoves anything that reminds her of Patrick to the back of her mind. The road curves slightly and lowers itself down a gentle hill. All the properties have rudimentary wooden gates.

"Come in, dearies. Welcome."

Standing at the top of the steps, a large, middle-aged woman clutching a greasy terrier in the crook of an ample, dimpled arm beckons to them.

"Mrs Whittaker," Seb shouts up. "My mother, Grace Lennox."

The dog snarls as Grace reaches up to shake hands.

The taxi driver clearly wants payment. She'll let Seb sort that out.

She follows Mrs Whittaker into the house. It smells damp and unclean. "In here," commands Mrs Whittaker pushing open the door to the front room. The furnishings are coarse, china knick-knacks litter every surface. Blackout material still hangs from the curtain rail, its outer folds faded and dusty. The netting covering the lower half of the bay window is torn and discoloured. Grace can see her luggage still on the pavement. "Seb. Go and get the luggage in." Seb leaves, grumbling. "This is lovely, Mrs Whittaker. Thank you so much for your hospitality."

The woman looks at Grace with ill-disguised hostility. It is clear they have nothing in common.

Seb takes off, claiming errands to be run. "I'll only be half an hour. I'll bring Ronnie back with me." She wishes he would stay and talk. Now that he is getting married, the opportunities may well lessen to almost nil.

Seb had never questioned why he had been sent back to the home country for the last few years of his schooling while his brother and sister had stayed in Rhodesia. He'd just seemed to accept it, not seeing himself as especially favoured or especially disadvantaged. Sorcha is different – more questioning, more uncertain, needing to know the correct code or the correct response for everything. She wonders if Seb rather than Nigel is in fact their greatest hope.

Grace sits at a low table on which rest tea things; mismatched and scored pyrex cups and saucers, a milk jug and metal tea pot. She has been left alone. Where is everyone?

At last there is a commotion in the hallway – Seb returning with Ronnie. Mr Whittaker appears too.

"Mother. I'd like to introduce you to Ronnie." They shake hands warily. "And Ronnie's parents, Greta and Arnold." Mr Whittaker, robust and jerky, leans over his wife's shoulder to vigorously shake Grace's hand. She is unsure whether to shake Mrs Whittaker's hand, having already done so on the doorstep. They smile at each other cautiously instead. Seb is on tenterhooks, pulling out chairs, tilting the milk jug, taking Ronnie's coat, obviously anxious that this meeting should go well.

"More tea, possibly, Mrs Whittaker?" Seb shouts out into the corridor. There is an answering crash from the back of the house and the smell of gas drifts in through the open door.

They are seated in a circle, tucked and tidy in their own individual isolation, when Mrs Whittaker appears with more refreshments. Seb sits, an ankle resting on his knee, one arm stretched along the back of Ronnie's chair, the other hand fiddling with the cuff of his sock. There is a smattering of dark hairs on his exposed calf. He seems impossibly grown-up yet still impossibly young. It is barely a few years since he was reading his tuppenny comics and collecting stamps of the Empire. And now, here he is, about to undertake a holy sacrament and, in doing so, ally himself – and the rest of his family – to the Whittakers.

To mask the rising awfulness of this encounter, Grace turns brightly to Ronnie. "Seb tells me you are training to be an *Engineer!*" Her voice is too shrill.

Ronnie reaches for a biscuit. "These are soggy."

"Hush, Ronnie," Seb whispers.

And what of Ronnie? Grace watches the girl as she meekly

balances a cup and saucer on her lap. What does Seb see in her? What *does* he see in her? A brutish hair cut atop a simple shift dress. Thick glasses. A man's coat. And, heavens, how could she not have noticed this before? One shoe stacked higher than the other. Oh, my goodness, Seb, she thinks to herself. You always were a rescuer. Why are you marrying this unprepossessing bit of a thing? Is she pregnant? Are you expecting a dowry? Has your father promised you money?

The bonds that are about to tie each person in this room to one another swirl around, thick and oily and suffocating.

The bluebottle rubbing its front legs and its back legs together on the edge of the biscuit plate seems to be exhibiting more glee than any of those present.

Chapter 12

March 1954

Sorcha
Craiginsch, Scotland

Sorcha stands at the back of the hotel, its granite bulk silhouetted against the silvering dusk. Wood smoke drifts down into the backyard from the high chimneys, like curious, benign wraiths. Through the sash windows, Marco is preparing supper for the golfers and the skiers returning from the last of the late winter's snow. Being Sunday, there will only be a handful. He sings to himself.

A startled cry pierces the thin night air – a duck disturbed by a water rat, perhaps. The wildlife is different here than in Africa, but the fight is bloody all the same.

She grinds her cigarette beneath the ball of her foot and pushes open the door into the warmth and humidity of the kitchen. Tapping Marco lightly on the shoulder as she passes behind him, to let him know that she is reporting for duty, she swings through the baize doors into the dining room. Marie is about to go off shift. "Don't do anything I wouldn't do!"

Sorcha laughs. She likes Marie. Marie is forthright, solid, to the point. "So. Did you ever, you know, kiss a blackie?" she'd asked Sorcha, shortly after she arrived at the Connaught Arms.

"Hush, no, Marie, I didn't. I'm not sure you're supposed to call them that these days."

"Are you sure?"

"Of course, I didn't."

"No, not that. Are you sure that you can't call them…you know? What are you supposed to call them?"

"I don't know. Negroes, perhaps. But that might just be in America. Goodness knows."

"Not sure I'd like to, somehow. Kiss one."

"Well, they probably think just the same about us."

"Yeah, suppose so. Not that you meet many up here anyway, in this unholy place. So, have you kissed anybody?"

"Marie! What a question!"

"Take it that's a no, then."

Sorcha shrugs. Marie has that same bright, inquisitive stare that her mother, Grace, has.

Sorcha's options on returning to England several months ago had seemed bewildering and banal. Despite being accredited and carrying a George Third tuppeny stamp and an embossed crest, it would appear that her qualifications from the Bulawayo Road Colonial School were not quite fit for a job with prospects in England. Pitman's Secretarial College on Bold Street had invited her to make a formal application later in the year. Daddy had written to a few of his relations and cronies. Then a letter arrived from Uncle Benedict in Craiginsch, Scotland with news of a general vacancy at the Connaught Arms. "Send the girl up by Friday week. Am sure we can put her to good use."

Marie's path to the hotel had been a little different. "Been keeping some stuff for a guy in Security at work. Said he'd been chucked out of his flat, landlord selling up, and he needed a place to store a few things for a couple of weeks until he got sorted."

Marie told her tale one night, sat on the edge of Sorcha's bed, her neck cricked by the sloping ceiling. A lone bulb picked out deep shadows in Marie's eye sockets, making her thin face even more skeletal. "Three o'clock one morning, the police come knocking with a search warrant and turn my place upside down. Turns out I'd been hiding a few thousands' worth of illegal weapons in transit to a hotspot in Africa. Near where you're from, I bet."

Sorcha listened, her mouth pinched with cynicism. How could Marie have got involved in such a business? Wasn't her story more likely a cover-up for a more humdrum reality – hard-luck stories being ten a penny in these straightened times?

"So, I've got a choice. Risk a going-over by the Glasgow Mafia for being an informant or risk a going-over by the authorities for gun smuggling. I'm charged with being an accessory, given bail and told to appear before magistrates the next day. No way, I tell myself. I'm getting out of there. That was four years ago. Been on the run ever since. Do a season here. Do a season there. One step ahead."

"Marie, you are funny."

Marie looked affronted. "Don't you believe me?"

"Well, why are you telling me this?"

"'Cos you look like someone I can trust."

"Like you trusted that guy in Security?"

"Yeah, you've got a point."

A long-case clock in the stone passageway chimes six. The front door opens to admit guests from the falling temperature outside, stamping their feet and pulling off their outer gear.

"Only six for dinner, including those two fellas who arrived this morning."

"Oh, those undercover agents," Sorcha jokes, playing on Marie's paranoia.

"You're taking the piss."

"Yep."

"I'm off duty now. You'll be alright, won't you, Sorcha?"

Sorcha nods. She enjoys working the dining room alone, enjoys the pace and challenge.

Standing at the French doors to greet the first guests, stiff and starched, the boundaries of her world are now the formal rooms of the hotel, the bar, the attic bedroom she shares with Marie, the short walk into town down the lane lined with rhododendrons, the post office, the coffee shop, the bus stop. Like mercury, confined yet free, fluid.

She likes to be busy, to attend to the minutiae of daily life in the hotel, to be an invisible pair of hands. She polishes and tucks and tidies, reunites guests with lost property, attends to the needy or distressed in the middle of the night.

She tells Marie nothing about the events of the final months in Rhodesia.

Maybe if on that gentle summer's day she had gone with Patrick in the plane, he might not have crashed. Maybe he was just performing some show-off routines as she watched from the lawn. Maybe – even – it would have been exhilarating beyond belief to watch the ruddy brown earth spin giddyingly towards them.

Would he have gripped her hand as the thousand small details – the propellers, the dials, the change in speed, in direction, the smell of fuel, the shift in gravity, the free fall of objects within the cockpit – all heralded the inevitable? Would he have looked at her and smiled? Would she have smiled back?

Would it have been horrific?

Or would it have been beatific?

In her dreams, she sees Patrick's handsome face glow golden and bright before the flames melt and consume his flesh; before his lips curl and roll back to expose his blackening teeth. She watches as his gloves pull away from his skeletal grip on the control wheel. And, curiously, she's happy for him. The dreams don't disturb her. She envies his blaze of glory.

But it's very different in the daytime. It takes a great effort of will to quell the panic and anxiety that seem to increase day on day.

"Good evening, Mrs Atkins. Mr Atkins." She greets the first of that evening's guests. "Let me show you to your table."

By eight o'clock, all the diners are seated.

"Cock-a-leekie soup for Table Three," Sorcha calls across the steamy kitchen to Marco. He grins and nods. "The two young men Marie's got her eye on?"

"The very same."

The two men tidy away an outstretched map from the table as she approaches. They have a certain familial look about them, related perhaps. It is more Marie's habit to scrutinise every visitor, in the hope that one day someone might walk in whose name is written on the same page as hers.

"How's he going to find you, this someone, if you keep moving about?" Jeanne had asked one night.

"How's he going to find me if I don't keep moving?" Marie replied wanly.

Is that how it works? Does one *have* to go on a search, hop up and down to catch Fate's eye? Is it not more seemly to…just…wait?

A small, fluttery movement from the table by the fireplace calls her over to the Atkins' table. "Yes. How can I help?"

"My wife would like some vinegar please."

"Certainly, sir." Mrs Atkins grips Sorcha's forearm, a lace handkerchief bunched in her hand.

"It is very hot in here. Don't you think so, my dear?"

"Don't make a fuss, Ethel."

"Oh, I'm not making a fuss, it's just that…" Mrs Atkins' bony hold becomes tighter and tighter. A musky smell rises from her small body, like geraniums or violets. "It's just rather…"

Sorcha glances at Mr Atkins who looks stern at the situation running out of his control. A red stain spreads across Mrs Atkins' chest.

"Would you like me to fetch a fire screen?" Should she address Mrs Atkins or Mr Atkins? Mrs Atkins nods once, twice, eyes down.

"Yes. Do that."

"Right you are, sir."

The other diners watch as she positions a screen embroidered with a stag between Mrs Atkins and the log fire, careful not to block any heat from Mr Atkins who, she is amused to note, is himself looking incommoded in a thick woollen jacket and tie.

She recognises her father in Mr Atkins who, dining in the restaurant before travelling back to Liverpool, had allowed Sorcha to unfold the napkin and place it in his lap while Grace gently slid hers off the table placing it on her own lap.

By ten o'clock most of the diners have left, the tables are set for breakfast and the kitchen cleared. Marco calls out goodnight as Sorcha switches off the lights. A shadow appears at the doorway.

"Uncle Benedict! You gave me a fright!"

"Never mind about that, lassie. Come into the bar. You've worked well tonight."

Sorcha does, in truth, fancy a drink. The village has its own distillery, run by another member of her father's disparate family. This is the only whisky sold in the bar, on Benedict's diktat. "Golden as frosted sun. Pungent as crushed heather. And as startling as your grandmother's ghost."

"That's very fanciful, Uncle Ben."

"Well, that's what we tell the trippers and we get a bottle of the 35-year-old stuff every Christmas." He pours a generous measure and slides the glass along the bar.

"Are you not having one?"

"No, never touch the stuff. Keep an eye on things down here and lock up will you?"

Sorcha nods, for a moment silenced by the fiery trace of her first sip. "Right-oh, Uncle."

In a dark corner of the bar, flanked by the two men from Table Three, sits Marie. Sorcha raises an eyebrow behind Uncle Benedict's back. Marie puts a finger to her lips.

"And keep an eye on young Marie too," he whispers as he passes her, sliding the bar door closed behind him.

"Sorcha! Sorcha!," Marie mock whispers. "Come over here. Bring your drink." Reluctantly, Sorcha slides off the bar stool and joins the group of three by the dying fire. "Has old Bennie Boy gone to bed?"

"Yes."

"Good. Then we can have some fun." Sorcha's heart sinks, but she smiles politely as Marie introduces her to her two companions. "Sorcha. I'd like you to meet Peter." She taps his knee, her hand sliding from his trousered leg as Peter stands to shake Sorcha's hand.

"Good evening, Sorcha. Very pleased to meet you. Your bubbly little friend here has told me so much about you."

Sorcha takes in the oiled hair, the strong scent of cologne and soft hands. This one will be Marie's chosen target, her mission for the night. He smells of money, shiny, new-minted money, the sort that could promise you anything you want, so long as you have goods to offer in exchange. Peter holds her hand a fraction too long. She feels herself blush under his scrutiny.

"And this is John, Sorcha. Sorcha, John!"

"Hello."

"Hello."

Peter sits down and replaces Marie's hand on his lap. She grins and raises her eyebrows at Sorcha. Maybe it wouldn't be too long before she and John are *de trop* and can leave.

Let the courtship begin.

Just the slightest pause, a brief rebalancing, before Peter and Marie both speak together. They laugh loudly and indicate the other to speak first.

"You go."

"No, you go."

"Oh, alright. If you insist." Addressing Sorcha as if speaking to the whole room, "I was just telling your charming friend Mary here…"

"Marie. I'm Mar-*ie*. And this is Sorcha."

"Yeah. Course. I was telling your charming friend, Mar-*ie*, here about London. It's not so bad now. Really picking itself up. Lots of opportunities, if you're prepared to work hard."

"So, what do you do then, Peter?" Marie's eyes are bright, drilling.

"Car sales. Showroom in Ealing. Boss looking to expand. Go further into town. 'I'm your man', I told him. Easy enough to buy up a few bombed-out plots. Everybody's got money these days. And if they haven't, it's their own bleedin' fault. Get ourselves a few stylish imports from the Continent and sell them on."

Marie nods emphatically. "Yeah, I can do paperwork. Even speak a bit of French…"

"We all need a bit of cheering up. Times have been hard," Peter thunders on.

"Parlez-vous Anglais?" Marie simpers into her drink.

"And, like I say to anyone who comes into the showroom, we need to do our bit for Queen and Country. Trade's the thing. That's what's going to take us through."

"Un. Deux. Trois."

"Wouldn't be surprised if we had a united Europe soon. Get rid of these trade tariffs."

"You even listening to me?"

"Cut tax right back. That's what needs to happen. Never mind paying back war debts…"

"I said, Peter, are you even listening to me?"

"What's that, duck?"

"Counting. In French, I was. I can speak French and I can do paperwork. I could help you."

"Yeah, well. Sure. That's lovely. I'm sure we'll get a chance to check out your talents at some point." Peter carefully places his drink on the table in front of him before sliding one arm along the bench seat behind Marie and blatantly undoing a button on her blouse with his other hand.

"Get off, you."

"You don't mind, do you?"

"Sure, I do."

"Sure, you don't."

"I'm a nice girl."

"I'm nice too. Aren't I, John? Do yourself up then, if you object."

Sorcha glances at John next to her. He is rolling the base of his glass around the outer edge of a water ring on the table.

"John. Tell the girls I'm alright. Harmless!"

"He says he's harmless."

"See!"

Marie fingers the open button on her blouse abstractedly. It might be that, upon this little button, the rest of her life will depend.

Just go steady, Sorcha silently urges her friend. Marie turns her attention to John.

"Are you in cars too, John?"

"No. I'm 'in' medical school."

Does John expect her to be as obliging as Marie? If he does, he is certainly a more circumspect player, barely lifting his eyes from the table.

"Where?" Sorcha asks.

"Sorry?"

"Where are you in medical school?"

"Oh. Middlesex."

"That's nice." She feels dumb and stupid so close to the intimate interplay of tension and expectation between Marie and Peter.

"What do you do?"

His question surprises her but before she can answer, Peter's voice loudly breaks into the silence, "That's how it is, is it? Not doing that cheeky little button up then? Well, how about I help its little fellow out. Oooh, looks like it's popped itself open all by itself!"

Marie glances at Sorcha over the top of Peter's head as he playfully waggles a finger between her breasts.

Ignoring John's last question, Sorcha mouths, "What are you doing? Be careful."

Marie nods and mutters, "I'll be alright."

Surely this sort of flirtation is best carried on in private. "I think I'll lock up and go to bed." John rises from the table too and stands while Sorcha extinguishes the lights. A small burning disc at the centre of the ashy fireplace is the only light in the room.

"Night night, lovers," Peter shouts.

Silently Sorcha and John leave the room. As Sorcha slides the bar door closed behind her, Marie laughs loudly.

"Night," Sorcha says, turning to climb the wooden back stairs.

"Night."

As John makes his way down the carpeted corridor, Sorcha wonders if he finds fault with her for leaving her friend in the bar. She wishes she could call him back, explain that such rapid and brutish courtships appal her too. But that Marie deserves a chance. The world is not a naturally kind or generous place and it might take a little self-promotion – strutting and preening – to change one's luck. This much she *has* learned.

Sorcha wakes at 05.30 as usual the next morning. Dawn is still a couple of hours away. She lies on her back for a few moments gathering herself for the day ahead. The early risers will be coming down to breakfast in an hour or so and the kitchen will already be lively with noise and warmth and steam.

A sound brings her attention back into the dusky bedroom. A stirring in the next bed. At least Marie must have made it back last night. She had tried to stay awake, lying uncomfortably on her right arm to keep her sleep shallow to check on Marie on her return, but sleep must have overtaken her.

She lifts her work clothes from her chair, the fibres cold and damp in the scant air and tiptoes out to the bathroom to get dressed. The light from the corridor cuts into the crepuscular denseness of the room. Peter is in the bed, his vast back shielding Marie. Sorcha stops in the doorway and stares. He is a white leviathan. She follows the folds of skin in his exposed back, the lines straight and angular. His skin is blotchy, sprinkled here and there with freckles and dark spots. He shifts slightly in his sleep and Sorcha closes the door hurriedly on an unnerving tableau of intimacy, ugliness, vulnerability.

She dresses in the cold bathroom, the half-tiled walls shiny with dampness, goose pimples emerging from every tender part of her body like quill beds. "Damn," as she realises she has left her watch in the room.

Tentatively she pushes open the bedroom door. The bed is empty, rumpled. Peter is dressed in a shirt and socks. Marie is skewered to the wall, her legs wrapped round his midriff. She slides up the wall with each of his thrusts. Both her hands grip her hair as she leans one elbow on his shoulder, the other bent arm flailing wildly. Their loud, guttural, rhythmic chant is tribal, primitive. Sorcha stands at the door, transfixed. There is no possibility of running to the sideboard to retrieve her watch and making her escape unnoticed. Yet she needs her watch for breakfast duty.

Marie's tightly closed eyes open, slowly, sultrily. She focuses on Sorcha, their eyes lock. "Alright, love," she drawls.

"Mm."

"Not you, idiot. We've got company."

Peter turns his head so that he too can see Sorcha.

"So we have." He hitches Marie higher. In doing so, his shirt tails lift above his buttocks. "Always room for one more."

Marie's face falls as she stares Sorcha out venomously. "I'm…I'm…just getting my watch." She runs into the room and out again as if chased by all the demons of hell. She slams the door behind her and leans against the corridor wall to catch her breath.

Voices came from within the room. "What do you mean, always room for one more?"

"Oh, don't make a fuss. Just having a laugh. Come here, you."

It is only as she serves breakfast that the implications of Peter being in their bedroom make themselves clear to her one-by-one. Not least, it is absolutely forbidden to invite anybody up to their accommodation. If Uncle Ben found out that Marie had taken a guest not only into the room but into her bed, he would be beyond livid. Unlikely that he would evict Peter and John, but she is absolutely sure that Marie would be ejected without pay and without references. Uncle Ben could be very unforgiving. Fired by a righteous anger, he would feel justified in cutting a member of staff loose, hamstrung, into the disaster of her own making. 'Well, you should have thought of that first, my girl'.

And what would Uncle Benedict say to her father? Would he be discreet, to spare his blushes, to not impute any responsibility to the father for the daughter's lack of morals? Or would he assume she was somehow involved and accuse her outright of being shameless?

Marie comes in to the dining room. Not a single detail betrays her guilt. She smiles to all the guests, neat and chipper as usual. But then, what did Sorcha expect for a transaction which, she presumes given the shabbiness of the location, was so very workaday?

"I want a word with you," Sorcha hisses as they pass in the swing doors to the kitchen. Marie waggles her fingertips as if without a care.

Following breakfast, Sorcha signals Marie to follow her outside. "Bloody hell, Marie. How could you do it?"

Marie stares back, brazen, hard. "None of your business what I do."

"Yes it is when it endangers both of us. You are a fool. How dare you bring a man to our room? How do you know you can trust him? For goodness' sake, I was asleep."

"Well, if you slept through it, no harm done is there?"

"I don't believe you. You are so stupid. I hope he's worth it but I'm pretty sure he won't be."

"Miss La-di-da who's never kissed a man. What do you know about it?"

Sorcha feels her heat rising. It is true. What does she know about it? That precious gift given to one's husband, according to her mother and the nuns – is it also a commodity outside the matrimonial bond? Is it a gift that could be given over and over, to different recipients? And what made it – sex – so special, so damn special?

The briefest glimpse of Patrick, his eyes narrowed, his lips parted, flashes into her mind. That weight on her chest, is it desire? Or is it sorrow at desire denied? "I may know nothing. But be careful. Don't give yourself away too easily."

"You're so prim and proper. You would say that. Anyway he's taking me out for dinner tonight. So shove that in your pipe and smoke it." Marie marches away, flinging her half-smoked cigarette into the bushes. "And don't you go bloody telling that uncle of yours either," Marie shouts before disappearing through the back door.

When Peter and John come down for breakfast, Sorcha cannot look Peter in the eye. How much of herself – her flesh and her secrets – had she unwittingly exposed to his gaze?

Marie hurries to their table, shimmering, with her pad in one hand, pencil in the other. "I'll get this," she says, pushing Sorcha out of the way. "Good morning, gentlemen. I trust you slept well."

"Tolerably well, thank you," replies Peter, concentrating on the breakfast menu. John nods briefly at Sorcha.

"Spot more golf today, is it, gentlemen?" Marie is bright, loud, breezy.

*

It is Marie's night off and Peter is taking her out. She has high hopes that something might come of it. "You never know. He might give me a gift. I've told him in so many words that I'd go anywhere with him, follow him to London, if he wanted. Just got to play my cards right."

That evening, John dines by himself. He only glances up to request water or when she removes his empty plates. Is he at all concerned at his partner's nightly wanderings? Embarrassment makes her clumsy. "Oh, I'm so sorry," she flusters as she overfills his water glass. She dabs the spreading liquid with a cloth before hastening away into the kitchen.

"What's the matter, *cara?*" Marco asks as she leans against the steel kitchen counter. "You ill?"

"No. Nothing's the matter. Just feel a bit queasy, that's all."

Marco pulls out a chair and tells Sorcha to sit. "No, I'm fine. Truly."

"You look startled. Sit!"

"Oh, you know. It's a bit warm and…and…I sometimes wonder…"

Marco hands Sorcha a glass of iced water. "What do you wonder?"

"Why life is so *dangerous*, I suppose. Risks. How far you have to go to get what you want in life. Deciding whether the risks justify the outcome." Marco nods and pulls a chopping board towards him, lining up strips of rosemary.

"Go on."

"Because nothing is certain. You don't know until you get so far into something what the ultimate price is going to be. And it could be way, way more than you ever want to pay." Skilfully and swiftly, Marco cuts the herb into small segments, dark green

104

circling the milky white centre. She watches, hypnotised by the action of his knife.

"And you can't go back." She raises her voice slightly. "You've compromised yourself too much. You've lost everything. Your ambition, your chance of success and whatever it was you had to sacrifice to achieve it." Marco stops chopping as Sorcha stops speaking. Oh, sweet Marie. Just what are you doing? The smell of chopped rosemary refreshes the air like the aftermath of a storm.

Images of Patrick flicker into her mind. It's not really Marie who has sold herself down the river though, is it? The smell of whisky blooms around her face. Patrick is looking down on her, his black eyes searching, searching for her consent. She feels his – she cannot name his part – nudging her upper thigh. "Are you ready?" he asks. She nods. The nuns said it would hurt. That pain is part of the blessed sacrifice. It does, but only briefly. This is disappointing; she wants to offer up her pain as a salve to his pain. She holds herself straight. Someone might hear them. It's over quickly. Patrick beside her, smoking a cigarette, offering her one. He stares at the ceiling, inviting no further intimacy.

"You're a crazy kid. I don't understand a word. To be honest, I don't hear a word. In my mind, you just give thanks to the good Lord for guiding you through another day, for your work and for your family. Enough, surely?"

"Yes, I suppose you're right." Sorcha stands.

"Cranachan for Table Five. Go!"

She pushes backwards through the baize door. John has gone.

The next day, the men leave the hotel.

"Be sure to come back soon," Sorcha mutters as they drive away.

"Shut up, you," snaps Marie. "That's not funny."

"So he didn't offer to take you with him then?"

"Leave off, will you!" Marie turns from the front door and walks at speed over the worn stone flags towards the service areas at the back of the hotel.

"No, I won't leave off." Sorcha charges after her, grabbing her arm. "You've been messing around, right under Uncle Benedict's nose. He'd sack us both if he knew what's been going on."

"Well, why don't you tell him then, Miss Goody Two Shoes? Save your own skin." Marie is defiant yet close to tears. An inky-red burst colours her face and neck. She turns to the wall as the Housekeeper walks past, curious yet nonchalant. Sorcha smiles over her shoulder and moves her relative position from one of challenge to one of protection.

"What happened to playing your cards right then last night?" she asks in a gentle tone.

"Anyway," Marie smiles. "You didn't help. Standing there, staring."

"I was not staring! It was a bit of a shock, that's all, coming into the room like that."

"Shock for both of us."

"Yes, well. Didn't think you'd come back."

"Oh, Marie." A wearying sense of futility mutes Sorcha's voice. "I am sorry."

"Not your fault, I suppose."

"No. I mean, I'm sorry that it all came to naught."

"Oh, I wouldn't say that. Had a good time, didn't I? Dinner. Night out. Didn't have to pay for a thing."

"It's just that the stakes seem so high."

"What do you mean?"

"That you had to, I don't know, give so much away for so little in return."

"What, like, all for the sake of a quick shag?"

"Well, something like that, I suppose. I know you were hoping that it would all lead somewhere. A ticket out of here. A job."

"Don't be soft. Never said such a thing."

"Yes, you did…"

"I know what these business types are like. Probably married for all I know. And it wasn't all 'for naught', as you say. Got dinner, didn't I?"

Sorcha can think of no further response. Marie had sold herself short. But it would serve nothing to humiliate her friend further.

"So how did you get on with John, when Peter and I were in town? We wondered whether he'd ask you for a drink or something. Peter told him to. You two seem quite well matched – both on the serious side."

Sorcha shakes her head. "No, no. He had his dinner. Barely said a word and then I guess he went up to his room. Didn't see him again all evening."

"Oh, well, never mind, dearie. One day you'll find out what all the fuss is about."

Chapter 13

May 1958

Sorcha
Thurstaston, The Wirral

The tide is out. Sea water collects in pools amongst the hard, ridged sand. From the clifftop she can see a few dippers reaching their beaks deep into the sand. A cold wind buffets the car, throwing droplets onto the windscreen. John turns a handle and the black rubber of the wipers scrapes noisily across the misted glass.

"Marry me."

John's proposal is more a suggestion, tentatively offered, than an absolute imperative.

She had been surprised to receive a letter from John two weeks after he and Peter had left the Connaught Hotel. He wrote of his plans for the future, once he had qualified in general practice from the Middlesex. He asked her what her plans were.

She replied, "I'm not sure. I've been put beyond the bounds up here in Scotland. Father found me the position but I am out of sight, out of mind. I should be making plans of my own, I know that. But I truly don't know where to go or what to do."

Subsequently, standing on the platform at Kings Cross station, waiting for her train back to Edinburgh, he'd grasped her shoulders and planted an inexpert kiss on her lips. She'd turned away quickly and pushed through the crowd without looking back. Sitting by the train window, as the brick-lined tunnels gave way to new housing and pasture, she'd caught her reflection and thought about that kiss. What did it pin on her? A contract? A promise?

She wouldn't mention Patrick to John. What could she tell him? That this man, briefly her lover, crashed out of the blue Rhodesian sky within her sight. That nightly she stands in the African bush and watches as rivets melt and metal panels fall away like opening petals. Behind billowing black smoke, his body curls and rises as if to greet her, before falling back again, all life spent.

She'll tell John she can't promise to love him. That cold white steel encases what was once a warm and tender heart.

He'd enquired whether Marie had in fact made it down to London to begin work in the motor trade, adding that, although he and Peter were cousins, other than a shared interest in golf, they saw little of each other.

Giving Sorcha a quick hug before leaving the hotel for good, Marie had whispered into her hair to go and fucking get laid and to, perhaps in contradiction, follow her dreams.

Maybe John was offering her a chance at both – within the sanctity of marriage.

Chapter 14

July 1962

Seb
Southport, Lancashire

"Darling. It is so nice of you to come." Grace waits for Seb to empty the boot of the car of his overnight bag and coat and climb the rough concrete steps to the front door of the bungalow. "No children?"

"Hello, Mum. No children."

"And Ronnie?" Grace peers round Seb as if to check that no family members are lurking.

"Sends her deepest condolences and apologies."

"Oh. I see." She turns into the hallway and shuffles towards the kitchen. "Never mind. I'll put the kettle on anyway."

"Mum! Come here!" Grace turns to him wearily and he folds her into his arms. She is thin beneath the ill-assorted layers of clothing. He can't remember ever really giving her a hug before and the thought of it shocks him. She struggles and he releases her instantly. "I'll put the kettle on."

"Ronnie sends these." Seb puts a bunch of yellow chrysanthemums on the draining board. A couple of petals fall off and float listlessly in the washing up bowl.

"Chrysanthemums! How…appropriate."

"Listen, Mum. Sit down and I'll make the tea."

"No, it's alright. I know where everything is. You sit down. You've had a journey."

Seb sits at the red topped kitchen table and watches his mother slowly assemble the cups and saucers. It takes all her concentration. There's a hole in the lino which she automatically navigates around in her slippers on her way to the tea caddy.

"Listen, Mum, I'm really sorry I wasn't there. I was in Frankfurt and by the time the hotel gave me the message…" A hold-up on the way to the finishing line, everyday accidents and triumphs mirroring the great race itself.

"It was quick, son."

"Sorcha – did she make it?"

"Yes. She was there."

"No chance, I suppose of Nigel…"

"No. Someone sent him a telegram. He telephoned, actually." She looks up, her face momentarily bright. "All the way from Wellington. It was like he was in the next room."

"That's good. Well, I'm here now."

"What's that you say?"

"I said, 'I'm here now'."

"So you are, son. So you are."

There is a long silence. Seb drinks the milky tea and wants to pick at the edging to the table. There are crumbs, hairs, debris caught in a sticky black line.

"Where's the oilcloth that used to be on this table?" Stupid question forced out of his mouth by the heavy silence.

"Tidied it away. Always hated it."

"Oh, but I liked it." It had been a present he and Ronnie had brought back from Stornoway – a fact seemingly forgotten by Grace.

"I might be able to find it for you again, if you wanted it."

"No. No. No. That's fine." Already the conversation has driven itself into the bank. He wishes he could find some words of comfort. He wishes, also, if somewhat childishly, that Grace would find some words of comfort to offer him. For the loss of his own father. However incomplete and shallow their relationship had been, Guy was still his father. She gazes into the porcelain cup. The hairs on the top of her head are becoming sparse. If he saw her in the street, he thinks, he might not recognise her, assuming her to be far older than her fifty years.

"Is there anything you'd like me to do?"

"No. We'll manage. Thank you."

We? Who is 'we'? A reflex born of thirty-two years of marriage? Or has Sorcha got it all sewn up?

"Good. Good. So, there's nothing you'd like me to do for you. You sure?" Grace nods. Another long silence ensues, till the question forms in his mind. He feels humbled, like a child before an inscrutable parent. "Do you want to go and visit Dad?"

"We can do if you like." Grace rises, collecting the tea things and putting them in the cold washing up water.

"Er..." No. Really he wasn't sure if he did want to. Yet again, the question had been squeezed out by the weight of so much silence.

"Come on. Get your coat. We can go now."

Oh shit.

The funeral parlour is in the same part of town. They sit on padded plastic seats in the window waiting to go in. The place is noisier than he might have expected. Out of sight, doors slam, water runs through pipes, a telephone rings. "Whenever you are ready." The undertaker comes through, pulling on his black jacket as he holds open the door for them. As they walk down the dimly lit corridor, someone switches on some music he recognises as Mendelssohn – vaguely churchy, vaguely uplifting. The tape warbles and squeaks before the music gets into its stride. A strong smell fills the corridor, like lavatory cleaner.

He ushers them into a small room. A brass cross sits in front of a small, raised translucent window. There are two chairs beside a low table with a box of tissues and a bunch of plastic lily of the valley. A coffin sits on a gurney alongside the wall. From his standpoint at the open door, he can see pleats of white satin and the backs of Guy's knuckles. He has never seen a dead body before.

Grace approaches the coffin and puts her hand inside to hold one of Guy's. She licks a finger and smooths his eyebrows. "Always had unruly eyebrows, your father." Seb smiles wanly. "Come. Come." Grace beckons him over.

"No. Mum. I'm…"

"He won't hurt you."

"I know, Mum. It's just…"

"He can't hurt you. He can't hurt a fly now."

Seb advances a step or two. He can see the right-hand side of the body, dressed in a tweed suit, thick brown brogues. He is curious now. Just what does a dead body look like? Just what does his father's dead body look like? Did life leave him peacefully, or did he fight the leaving of it with every last breath? What would he see on his father's face?

Grace reaches out her hand and pulls Seb towards her. "See." It's hard to resist her pull.

Seb looks in. It's curious, like looking down on a child's cradle but, grotesquely, there's an aged man lying there. Not even one that looks like his father. The cheekbones are too prominent, the eye sockets too bruised, the lips too stretched. No way to tell if he surrendered happily or if it was all on Death's terms.

What should he do? Should he offer a prayer for the safe keeping of his father's soul? Mumble thanks? Kiss him? There are no clues. For his entire life, he had always responded to his father's lead. Question and answer. Statement and response. Ronnie always said they were like schoolmaster and pupil in detention.

Grace busies herself around the body, straightening his cuffs, pinching his cheeks, retying his laces. Seb sits and watches Grace move easily through her macabre rituals.

She mutters a few words and goes to stand in front of the closed door. This must be the signal to leave. He reaches past her to pull on the door handle. She walks through the door and waits for him in the corridor. She links her arm through his and he wonders whether it would be appropriate to ask if there was anywhere they could wash their hands.

Back at the house, they sit while dusk gathers around them. The phone rings in the hallway, but Grace ignores it. This house is unfamiliar to Seb. It could be a stranger's house, with just a few recognisable totems of a previous life – an antelope's head, a petrified elephant's foot serving as a doorstop, a couple of oil paintings – a tall church spire, a cricket scene, children on a wall.

"These are nice." Seb rises to look closer.

"Thank you."

"Did you do these?," he asks in surprise, spinning round to face his mother.

"Yes. Went to afternoon classes. For a few years." Seb leans in to study them a bit closer. Oils – a murky grey-green with strong lateral strokes. Pin points of colour – orange, red, ochre. A series, maybe? How come he didn't know?

"What…exactly…" He points to the largest canvas.

"The view from the coast, as the ships breach the Mersey.

You can see the buoys, lighthouse, the Anglican cathedral, the dockyards." As he looks closer, he can make out blocks of sandstone, criss-crosses of metal, an obelisk like structure all dimmed and obscured by a thick, deadening fog. "Your father didn't like them. Said they weren't very cheerful. Surprised he let me hang them up really."

"Listen, Mum. Are you going to be alright? I mean, for money?"

"Oh, I expect so. Not that there will be much spare," she says hurriedly, defensively. "Why? Do you need some?"

"No, Mum. I don't. We're fine. Just wanted to make sure you were."

She shuffles slightly in her seat and looks tired. There is no way that Grace would complain about lack of money. Whatever is left to her following Guy's death would just have to suffice. She would make do, even to the point of hunger, with what Guy has provided.

She has fallen asleep, as might a bird, delicately, unobtrusively.

Did she know of their meeting two years ago?

Guy had written, asking if Seb wanted to join him on a sure-fire venture. Guy had the contacts; all he needed was a few quid up front, 'seeing as you are doing so well with that marine engineering company of yours'. They had arranged to meet at the Adelphi. 'On no account tell your mother. Or that wife of yours.'

They sat in the lea of the grand piano, china cups and a silver coffee pot between them. "Chappie I know out in Bulawayo says he's got lists and lists of antiques and treasures appropriated by the Nazis during the war. A lot of them went into state museums in occupied territories. After all, where better to hide something than in plain sight?"

His father talked enthusiastically about the opportunities to make money reuniting lost treasures with their rightful owners. "The Germans were fanatical about inventories. They stripped out chateaux, loges, hotels, museums, catalogued and crated these works of art. Some went to the privileged few within the Reich, others were put aside in the Jeu de Paume in Paris to fund future war work or rehabilitation after the war when, presumably, Germany had taken over most of Continental Europe.

"Said this list was 'spoils of war'. Think he picked up a few mementos after the liberation of Tobruk in '43. Taken him fifteen years to look at them properly. He says collectors would pay good money, no questions asked, for proven provenance."

"But I thought a lot of stuff had been returned."

"Yes, it has. But only where ownership can be established. A lot of paintings, modern ones particularly, were considered immoral, degrading and so were dispersed throughout Europe and North Africa. Others are missing, presumably still in storage somewhere. If we can find the owners..."

"If they are still alive."

"Yes, or their descendants, then we can earn quite a nice 're-introductory' fee."

Guy was leaning forward in his seat, a gleam in his eye. "Obviously there will be a few expenses that need to be met before we can, you know, declare our hand."

"And that's where I come in?"

"Just wondered if you wanted in, that's all." What was his father offering him? An opportunity to get rich? Or an opportunity to take part in a hare-brained scheme that was at best dodgy, at worst ridiculously illegal?

It felt strange to be sitting across from this man, his father, in a position of relative equilibrium. This was the first time Guy had ever wanted anything from him other than the obeisance of a dutiful son.

"How much do you want?" Doubtless his father would see this as a return on their long-term investment in their youngest son's education.

"Just a couple of thousand."

"Pounds?" Seb could not keep the dismay from his voice. Guy looked immediately punctured.

"Or anything else you care to put in."

"Dad. I have no spare money. Any that I do have has to go right back into the business."

"But you are always saying how well your business is doing. Not as if you have that many commitments. And if that pathetic wife of yours bothered to get herself a job…"

"Dad!" Guy sat back in his chair. "That is actually none of your business." The look of exhilaration had gone from his father's face as his eyes narrowed and jaw clenched. Seb felt his guts turn to liquid. This was possibly the first time in their thirty year relationship he had answered back. "Listen, Dad. I'm sorry. Grateful, obviously, that you thought to ask me."

Guy sprang to the edge of his seat, a red-black rage colouring his face. He grabbed Seb's wrist. "Listen, son," he hissed. "Don't make me beg."

"I…I… Dad. Let go. You are hurting me."

Guy roughly shoved his hand away and rose to his feet. "I knew it was a bloody mistake. Like you were a bloody mistake." He kicked the coffee table away and it skittered a yard or so along the black and white tiled floor. Seb watched a large brown stain quickly spread itself into the damask tablecloth. His father's voice sounded angrily from the cloakroom before he swung out through the hotel doors and was gone. Silently two waiters restored the table and tidied away the broken cups. "More coffee, sir?" Seb shook his head.

He had been a fool to respond to his father's letter in the first place. What pathetic hopes of a rapprochement had brought him to the Adelphi? What did his father mean that he was 'a mistake'? Was there more to that than just the desire to wound? He gazed at the red weals on the underside of his wrist. A family branding.

What was more shocking – to have been momentarily in the ascendant or to have been so rudely and finally dropped? A shock to realise that his father was short of money and asking his now-reviled son for cash. Surely the art works scheme was a massive figment of a slowly distorting mind. And what right did Guy have to profit from the war? Born in the last year of the nineteenth century, too young to enlist in the first war and tied to a desk job in the second before scuttling off to Africa while everyone else bent themselves to the post-war rebuild.

Three nail-shaped crescents had formed in the tender skin of his wrist. His veins bulged and pumped.

They had not set eyes on each other since the Adelphi, at least two years earlier. He'd persistently met Grace's gentle encouragement to visit with excuse after excuse. Ronnie's third miscarriage. Work commitments. The heaviest snow forecast since 1953. And so the years had drifted by.

The thought of it shames him. Redirected anger was ever his father's strategy. Punish not the offender but the weakest. As if the vulnerability of his wife, of his children, Seb among them, brought out the worst not the best in the man.

On occasions, he feels his father's blood rise in his own veins, and it horrifies him. Not that he would lay a finger on Ronnie but her vulnerability has acquired another hue lately. Is she punishing her body for the punishments it had meted out to their marriage? Bizarrely, it is as if all her vitality is passing to those objects around her – her thinness given up to the corpulence of the sofa, her colour leached to the garish plastic jewellery she wears, a little bit of her vitality leaving each time somebody opens and closes the front door. She looks brittle, dried out.

In the early days, his heart had melted for the fragility of her. Now, if he is honest, most of his compassion has leached away. He wakes in the night, drenched in sweat, just at the imagined point of snapping her neck with his thumb pressed hard under her chin or peeling her yellow flesh in strips from her yellow bones.

Christ, he could do with a joint.

Seb stays for two days, offers to tidy away some of Guy's things for this might allow some insight into his late father's affairs, to find out if Grace will be able to support herself, but Grace is adamant that nothing is to be touched.

The house must stay as it is, at least for the time being. Small, poorly made, draughty, more a refuge from misfortune. Hunkering down low behind the windblown dunes of the Lancashire coast, strafed at night by the light from the lighthouse, echoing to the lonely call of ships' horns.

She looks so gaunt, like Ronnie. A strange sense that Grace is mourning more than Guy's death comes to him, that she is already practised in the art of grief. She seems to stand so at ease in the midst of the fast-flowing river.

He really must make an effort and come and visit more often. Bring the family.

Chapter 15

September 1965

Sorcha
Thornton Hough, The Wirral

There is a small face staring solemnly from the bottom of the bed. Short dark hair. Spiky. It must be the child. Wicker snaps as its small feet try to gain purchase on the blanket box. It tumbles silently to the ground, taking the folded laundry with it. That will have to be sent back downstairs for refolding.

She turns her head to the window. A bright stripe of light pushes between the parted curtains. Is it morning? There is no pain. Why has John not made the bed before leaving for work? Where has the pain all gone? She lies accused by the sunshine. Bugger off sunshine.

Again the small face appears, moving round the perimeter of the bed. A self-propelling head, floating towards her like a balloon. Tiny hands scuttle their way along the edge of the counterpane – counterpain – towards her. Some grotesque thing.

She stares into the bright light and then back at the advancing creature which is now no more than a small, dark shadow on her retina. It has an insistent pull on the bedcovers. Get off! Get off! They're mine! Why didn't John tuck her in? Keep her safe? She tugs the covers sharply towards her and the small body with the large head and the tiny, podgy, grasping hands disappears. There is a thud and a cry.

She'll have to tell Aya to fold the laundry. The bedclothes are still now but the sound of crying is frying her brains. "Shut up!" Her own voice is cracked, broken open by the oncoming force of the wail from the floor. Shut up, she croons. Shut up, little one. Mummy loves you. Mummy does love you, doesn't she? Mummy love. Mummy doesn't love you. Mummy. Doesn't. Love. You. Capiche?

She moves her head to the centre again. In front of her another sun-bleached, scored and scratched figure. Ah, Aya. "Aya." Aya bends to pick the child from off the floor. They are one. She lifts her hand to stroke its cool flesh but her arm is heavy and falls back onto the bed.

"Come on, Toby. Let's leave your Mummy alone."

It has no nappy and its tiny penis rests bulging on Aya's arm. The end seems to be feeding from Aya's arm. The skin on its testicles is like a prematurely hatched bird's, pink, lined, unlovely. Why should she feed such an ugly thing?

What is Aya saying? If she lies here long enough, they will all go away.

She is alone now. The bed is shaking. Her legs dance like a dervish, scattering sand and ash.

Chapter 16

January 1974

Grace
Southport, Lancashire

Don't know why we have to call this the 'Morning Room'. Possibly one of Guy's little affectations. Left over from our days in Rhodesia. That's called something different nowadays too. The country, that is.

You might possibly think a Morning Room would catch the early light but it is at least lunchtime before the place warms up. It is damnably cold in here.

Have we had lunch yet?

Grace eases herself slowly off her chair, a small side plate falling unheeded from her lap onto the floor. The rubber ferrule from her walking stick chips the edge of the plate, splintering the porcelain and leaving a powdery white residue in the ornate carpet. She heads for the fireplace.

She runs her fingers along the mantlepiece as best she can for her hand shakes, rotating manically from the wrist. Framed faces smile out at her.

They are all quite presentable in their way, the children and the grandchildren. Possibly Seb has the upper edge in the looks department. Eyes rather too hooded for complete trustworthiness. Broad-chested liked his father. Rather inclined to melancholy. Wrote long screeds from boarding school about missing home and asking after Mickey the tortoise. Might have been better if the school had put a stop to that.

She could ease the photographs from their frames to read the names on the back but does not trust her hands. Who is who?

Hands. Hands going tap, tap, tap. A young boy's voice, "Mother. Mother. Mother!" What does that child want? Nigel. She mustn't pull her arm away but sometimes it is all really too irritating. He is too insistent on his needs, that boy.

At least they all escaped Aunt Maud's nose. A 'monstrous proboscis' Guy had called it. Grace laughs. Yet he had been terribly offended when one of the boys had screamed his little head off when he first saw Maud. They all stared so. Sorcha saved the day when she climbed up on Maud's knee and made much of her pearls.

There is a brisk knock on the door. "Enter." Ah, the help. "Would you be kind enough to ring for Jacob for me and tell him I want a cup of tea?"

"The tea trolley will be round shortly, Mrs Lennox. Come and sit down and let me put a blanket round you. Your window is wide open again. You must be freezing. Come along, there's a good girl."

A firm hand presses into Grace's back and guides her to her chair. It is useless to resist.

"Are you helping Jacob today? You must be from the same village."

"Yes, that's right, Mrs Lennox. Now, let me tuck you in. That's better."

"Guy always said he could sell coals to Newcastle that one?"

"Who's that, then?"

"Why, Seb, of course. There was that day…" Grace stops to pull a handkerchief from her cuff. A wet cough fights its way out of her thin chest. "That day, ha ha, he persuaded Kitty Simpkins's chauffeur to drive to a liquor store and buy two cartons of cigarettes. Chesterfields. Cool as a cucumber he gave a carton to Clive Simpkins. Must have only been about twelve years old. Said something like, 'Here you are, sir'. Clive took it, of course and gave Seb five dollars for going. I asked him afterwards where he got the money from in the first place and he said, 'Jacob'. Your relative, presumably. Poor man stumped up a week's wage. We told Seb to return the money."

"And did he?"

"Doubt it." Grace watches the woman fussing around her room. "What's your name?"

"Belinda."

"Belinda." Grace ponders the name briefly. "We sent Seb back to England to finish his schooling. He was our big hope. Nigel was off like a shot, as soon as he could. He used to tap, tap, tap my arm, you know, when he wanted something. Very irritating."

Belinda does not keep still either which is also irritating. Her plastic apron rustles with each movement. Is it absolutely necessary to empty the waste bins so many times a day? Really, that woman might stop clanging the bin lid against the wall with her big clumsy foot on the pedal. It will mark the wall and we were told that when we vacated the house in Salisbury we would have to leave it in the pristine condition we found it. It was a nightly sport for the children, and Guy, to knock the mosquitoes and the cockroaches out against the wall.

"We left in such a hurry that I don't suppose we gave a moment's thought to cleaning. Funny, there was this dried-up orange under the sideboard in the dining room. Shrunk to the size of a golf ball, twice as hard.

"Three children we had. All born in Liverpool. It hit Sorcha hardest of all. I mean, she was very protected at school. Nothing more than a ramshackle colonial house in the Parliament district. Miss Griffiths was the headmistress. Welsh woman. God knows how she ended up there. Think there was something funny going on about the money."

Grace's eyes return to the photographs on the mantelpiece. There is one that draws her eye every time.

"He was always my favourite. I know you're not supposed to have favourites. But between Nigel's hurry to be off over the horizon and Sorcha's rather feeble ways, Seb was always the one to make me laugh.

"Have I told you how he persuaded Jacob to stump up five dollars for two cartons of cigarettes? Sold one carton to Clive for the price of two and pocketed the profits. Should imagine poor old Jacob went without many luxuries that week!"

Belinda is rubbing down the paintwork around the door. Grace stares at the flapping cloth, wincing at the squeak of the cloth against the gloss paint. She is concentrating. "I don't actually think you were in Rhodesia, were you?"

"No, ma'am."

"Well, why did you say you were?"

"I don't believe I did, ma'am."

"Well, anyway, Sorcha was very pretty. I'll say that for her. But she had this sort of fragility about her. That's why it affected her so badly."

"What affected her?"

"Why, the crash, of course."

"Of course."

Belinda moves from eradicating the fingerprints on the door to refreshing the water in the flower vase and filling Grace's water jug.

The crash. A croak escapes from Grace's throat. She delicately empties her mouth into her handkerchief.

Grace casts over her shoulder, her vision wavering with each unsteady shake of her head, giddyingly, disorientatingly. "We went on a leopard hunt, you know. When we first arrived. Hired some bicycles. Went out into the bush. Ha ha. The boys thought we might get kidnapped by bandoleros. Guy pointed out that we were very unlikely to be taken away by *Spanish* bandits. Bit foolhardy, I know. But we cycled to a rocky outcrop. Sat there for a while in the baking heat. Without any water or protection. And then we cycled back. But I saw one. I know I did. Or a tail at least, just the briefest switch before it was snatched from view. Think that was the highlight of living out there. That tiny, *tiny* glimpse."

But Linda is nowhere to be seen. Doors slam and voices shout further down the corridor. Grace returns her gaze to the African violets on the windowsill. They are dusty. Maybe Jacob might freshen them up when he's back.

That night, another person comes to put Grace to bed. This one doesn't have a black face. She has a small, pale face, no lips. Golden light shines through the closed curtains onto the counterpane. Is it really bedtime?

"Yes, it is, Mrs Lennox. Now, lie down, there's a good girl."

"What's this contraption here?"

"It's for your pain relief, and to help you get a good night's sleep."

"What's your name?"

"It's Katya, ma'am."

"Katya? I thought it was something else."

"No, it's definitely Katya. Would you like a sip of water?"

"No. I'll ring the bell if I need anything in the night."

"That's right. Night night."

"Goodnight."

She wants to sleep but there is a bolus of energy in her knees, her hips, her ankles. It twitches and pulses, making her legs dance. Her legs bend and draw upwards, knees to her chin. The plastic bed sheet rustles as she slides her feet, soles down, to the bottom of the bed again. Slowly she repeats the manoeuvre until the energy dissipates, along with the dull ache in her guts.

She waits for Patrick by night.

She is waiting by the fountain in the park. There is a babble of voices, the smell of ice cream wafers, a greasy smudge on the ground. Yet there is no one there. The park is empty. No, wait! Here he is. He's walking towards her. In uniform. He *did* come.

She rises from the bench and he takes her hand, lacing her fingers between his. His touch is electrifying.

They walk slowly down the drive towards the statue. He's not looking at her, so she can't look at him. Why doesn't he say something?

His pace picks up as they approach the monument. From the ground, the horse's bronze buttocks look massive and powerful above thin, bent legs. The rider, Viscount Combermere she seems to remember, is in full battle dress, rising out of the stirrups and waving a feathered hat in the air. Both rider and horse are snarling. Patrick leads her round to the darker side and pushes her against the cool plinth. He is pressing her hard. He is kissing her.

She must stop this dream. She must stop this memory. Oh, but, just a little longer.

He had stopped that young boy from tumbling full-charge down the park steps on his bicycle. But for Patrick stepping in, the youngster would have dashed his brains out or mangled his tiny limbs around the bike frame. Everyone thought the crash was Sorcha's tragedy. But what of *her* tragedy? She'd come home and found Kitty and Guy *post flagrante*. Not that she cared over much about that. Kitty minded. Not quite best friends, but close enough. Probably thought she was making amends by inviting Sorcha up to Collinson's Ridge to work. Perhaps Guy had put her up to it. No, that wasn't it. That's not why she wants to go back to the park. In her dreams. In her mind – that day. He'd caught up with her as she was walking away. His black, black eyes. She couldn't stop herself being drawn in to them. Stupidly, she'd told Patrick about Kitty's place. Had he gone there, hoping to meet her? Her? Not Sorcha. Her!

She would never have left Guy. He needed her. For all his bluff and bluster and brutalism, he was lost and he was lonely and she was his salvation, she knew that. His Rhodesian dreams thwarted. Home to yet another banal desk job. But the threat of violence was always there. Whatever happened to Jacob?

She couldn't openly grieve Patrick. Unlike Sorcha. Grief became a black, tarry mass in her heart. In her quiet times, she remembers him. Counts out their few, brief encounters like shiny pennies. She fingers and rubs each one, turning them over and over in her hands till they shine like new. And then swallows them down again to keep them safe, to keep them hidden.

She looks on for a little longer and then separates them and watches them part.

Patrick walks briskly one way.

Herself – twenty years his senior – walks the other way, the relief letters of the inscription on the plinth showing as indents in the pink and yellow skin of her bare shoulder.

Patrick! Wait for me! It won't be long now. I'm on my way.

Chapter 17

March 1975

Seb
Hope Mountain, North Wales

He wakes after a fitful night's half sleep. A grey wash penetrates the open weave curtains, dawn light smudging the disordered outlines of the bedroom. Damp permeates the cottage, chilling the rumpled bedclothes, casting a sheen over his naked body. He notes, with a hint of satisfaction, that his penis is not stuck fast, amoeba-like, to his balls but is rising to the scent, in blind purposefulness. He kicks the bedclothes further down the bed and runs his hand over his tentative erection.

Maybe it is last night's booze, maybe it is the fact the air is bloody freezing but his erection contracts fast, folds and ridges of surplus skin multiplying and deepening, colour intensifying, as his penis returns to being the useless nub it usually is.

What does it matter, anyway? His body is spare now, no excess baggage. His frame has lost the pudginess of excess, the markers of his previous life. The yearly increase in collar size, the demeaning tug on the belt. Gone. The dyspeptic discomfort of business lunches and boozy afternoons, chasing the contracts. Gone. Golf, the false bonhomie, strip clubs. Gone.

Although it would be better if his virility had not disappeared along with his midriff.

He rises off the bed and stands face on to the dusty cheval mirror. Sun rising over the Cambrian hills brings a tinge of gold. Rainbows twinkle in the bevelled edge of the glass. His skin loses its grey hue and begins to shine. Individual hairs stand sentry in the cold air, glint. Golden boy.

A cloud passes in front of the sun or it hasn't got the energy to lift itself above the horizon. Either way, the momentary wash of bright light disappears and the cottage returns to its cluttered, shabby self.

He'd taken the smallest room as his when he arrived at the cottage three years ago. At the time he thought to scrub some of the dark specks of mould off the inside of the dormer window, fix the curtain rail, hammer down the more perilous floor boards. But he hasn't. Nigel had made it a condition of living here, rent free, but the deal hasn't come to much.

One day he'll get round to it. If he stays. If the booze and the weed and Magda don't finish him off completely.

He needs a piss.

The door frame onto the landing is low and he has to bend. On the wall at the turn of the stairs is a large-faced pendulum clock, apparently from a nearby mine clerk's office. He'd tried to wind it up, get it started again, but the hands were frozen at 07:23.

He stumbles down the last few wooden steps, cursing as his fingers twist, trapping themselves between the last two spindles. An involuntary bead of moisture jolts to the end of his dick. And then another.

Making his way towards the back door, he slams open the panelled lavatory door. It crashes against the distempered wall.

The enamel light-pull swings jerkily over the dry, blackened pan. A bird dances on the outer window ledge, startled by the sudden noise, its ragged shape smudged by the translucent dimpled glass. What would it take to reconnect a water supply to this scummy place? He's fed up of relieving himself in a bucket.

Still naked he pushes open the flimsy back door. A magpie flies off, its wing feathers and tail feathers extended like close-quartered blades; it hops once, twice on landing a short distance away, as if no more bothered than the low-rise sun or Seb himself. The corner of the step darkens under the dribble of his undirected urine.

March in a remote cottage in North Wales is too cold to stand long at the back door. A shimmery haze covers his skin giving it, in the rain-washed light, a mother of pearl sheen. Could he be growing an exoskeleton? That would be awesome. Or – and Seb roots deep in his misfiring brain to find a handle on this new concept – is his skin about to sucker in under his skeleton? Sub-dermis. Sub-cutaneous skin? Sub-sub-skin. Skin that is not skin. Skin like chicken skin. Not the bluey-white-yellowy skin of a butcher's carcass but the bag with the giblets fastened with a closely pinched metal clip. What's happening here, babe?

He touches his forehead. His body temperature is still high. God, is he still tripping?

Butcher's carcasses. Hanging upside down in the trees on bent metal hooks are scores of fat naked men, their aprons hanging over their anonymised faces, their genitalia pointing listlessly to the ground.

Seb shakes his head and pain zigzags between his temples. Christ, he is!

Where is Magda? She'd brought the stuff with her when she arrived yesterday. She's not looking particularly good on it.

In fact, he'd barely recognised her when she stepped off the train. Like greeting a crone. He'd bent to kiss her cheek, muttering 'Hello, Crone' to himself as he applied his reluctant lips to her dry, powdery skin. She'd pulled his face to hers, the flat of her palm against the back of his neck.

"What you say?"

"Nothing! Hello." Her breath was stale.

She took a while to hoist herself and her belongings into the passenger side of the van. "Still got this old crate, then?"

"Mmm." He could hardly speak to her. It was as if she'd sent a poorly-modelled deputy in place of her previously lush, buxom self.

"What's up?" she asked, jabbing his forearm with her knuckles.

"Nothing. I'm just concentrating on driving, is all."

Magda nodded and grunted. On the half hour drive to the cottage, he pointed out landmarks. Little seemed to grasp her attention away from rifling in her duffle bag and the storage compartments of the van within her reach. This was getting deeply invasive and irritating.

"What exactly is it you're looking for?" She turned her head to him beakishly.

"Nuffin.'"

"Well, would you mind just sitting still, please. It's very distracting."

With exaggerated care, she stowed her hands in her lap and stared straight ahead. Within a minute or two, she was back to kicking the underside of the glove compartment like a petulant child.

They haven't seen each other for years. A postcard of Sofia, presumably bought in Bulgaria but posted in London, had arrived a few days earlier announcing her intention to visit. Three trains from Shrewsbury had come and gone before she stepped onto the platform. She recognised him before he recognised her.

To distract his attention away from the insistent tapping of her foot, Seb asked, "So, what have you been doing?"

"A bit of this. A bit of that."

"Enigmatic as usual."

"Don't be like that!"

"I'm not being like anything." Christ, what has happened to this woman? Five years earlier, they had spent the summer chasing clouds and dropping acid along Pennsylvania, Wisconsin, Minnesota, South Dakota, Wyoming, Colorado, Utah and Nevada to California, sleeping under the stars, shooting at rattlesnakes, grinding away to the sounds of The New Riders of the Purple Sage and the Grateful Dead. It was well beyond his powers of imagination to think of doing any such thing now with this woman next to him.

She had fallen asleep before they reached the cottage, her head nodding, chin on her chest. Thin tendrils of greasy hair imperfectly hid her crumpled face. A memory flashed up – watching her dance to 'Hello Mary Lou', performing to half a dozen truck drivers, her bare heels flashing whitely over the beer sodden boards of a roadside bar. God, he had wanted her that night! He remembered neon bursts over her bare flesh as she yowled like a wildcat on the floor of the van.

"We're here," he'd announced, roughly shaking her shoulder.

"Huh?"

"At the cottage. Get out."

Magda dragged her duffel bag behind her up the garden path to the splintered front door. Without pause, she walked straight in. Was she going to ask him for money? Good luck with that one, he thought, although he would surely split whatever he had with her.

She stared wide-eyed around her from the sofa, the corner of the crocheted-square throw lapping at her shoulder. He handed her tea, avoiding her fingers as she reached to grasp the cup.

For hours he watched her sleep, wondering why she had come. After all they hadn't seen each other for four years, Magda opting to try her luck in London while he returned to Liverpool to build some bridges with Ronnie. That hadn't worked, other than pretty much emptying his bank account in her favour and paying off Grace's long overdue nursing home fees.

Was he happy to see Magda? Old habits die hard. She was always the one who could squirrel out a supply of White Lightning, liquid hash or finely-cut fresh green kif. He was sure she wouldn't disappoint. He'd just have to wait till she woke up.

Maybe he should tidy up a bit and cook her a meal.

Darkness was pressing thickly against the bare windows when she woke, startling him by coughing at the doorway into the kitchen. She was holding the multicoloured throw around her thin shoulders.

"I'm starving. What you cooking?"

"Beans, chillies, brown rice, tomatoes, herbs."

"Not eaten in three days. But…I do have the perfect accompaniment." She unwrapped a small screw of tin foil and placed four white tablets on the table.

"Magda! My girl!"

Over dinner she spoke of the refugee she'd come across in Muswell Hill, a former experimental psychiatrist in Bulgaria doing state-sponsored research into induced psychosis. He'd fled the regime but held on to a few essentials on his route across Europe.

"Is that where you're living now? Muswell Hill?"

Magda nodded. "Kinda. Keep getting moved on. We're in this old carriage works at the moment. It's all boarded up, obviously. There's about twenty of us now, squatting. Easy pickings to be had, outside the tube station, off the street vendors. Not much of a life, I know, but, hey…" She looked around at the stone walls blackened with smoke and stained with algae, "… doesn't look like you're doing much better here."

He felt instantly and profoundly defensive of both the cottage and of Nigel's generosity in lending it to him. "This place is alright. A project, you know, for me to work on. Nigel's in New Zealand, of course, but… Not got round to doing much just yet, but it's better for being lived in, you know." Magda's doubtful face reflected back his own inadequacy. "Well, you know how it is. Will get round to it one day. Anyway, what about we take a transcendental hit?"

"Sure." Magda reached into the middle of the pine dining table for the tabs while Seb threw more logs on the grate. They'd learned from their experiences of taking LSD they were better, if not alone, then disentangled. Magda sat on the slate floor, leaning against the sofa while Seb pulled a high-backed chair within the dancing light of the fireplace so their respective trips wouldn't intertwine or interfere. Although it would be at least an hour before the benign effects of the chemicals made themselves known, they liked to welcome the warm onrush calmly and safely.

"Got no stereo, then?," Magda enquired, looking into the dusky corners of the room before gloomily announcing, "Reality sucks."

"No." She had a point though. Colours are brighter, the patterns more compelling, the visions more moving for a background of music. They would have to trip-toe in silence.

He can't remember the landscape of his acid trip in any detail. How had he even got to bed? Beneath the remote sense of primitive well-being, despite the odd creatures hanging in the trees, he is feeling absolutely fine. But where is Magda? Last time he saw her, she was staring into the dying fire with a beatific look of awe on her face.

She is not in the sitting room nor in the guest room. Certainly not in his bed. No invitation given and none accepted.

Maybe she had opted to take a walk over the fields. She operated between two points. Always needing someone to leave and someone to go to. Maybe that was what this visit was about. She was not so much journeying here as leaving there. Close-quartered in the van, driving east to west across the States, past lumber forests, salt lakes, high peaks, old railroad tracks, she often disappeared for hours on end. He'd learned to wait for the sun to set, the fairground lights to go out, tides to wash in and wash out. She always came back in the end. She was at her worst if untethered at one end. No child of the sky, she. Unlike Ronnie, who was quietly and stoically brave and needed no one, Magda played tag with everyone.

Seb returns to the kitchen dressed in jeans and checked shirt. The lino floor is sticky beneath his bare feet and the table still set as if both had just risen after supper. A handful of gorse is tied with string and placed in the middle of the table, together with a folded note. "For you. I'm off," it reads. Seb peers through the fly-blown kitchen window for maybe one last glimpse. She might be following the drovers' path over the brow of the hill and, sensing his distant gaze, turn and wave before thumbing a lift from a passing car. But no.

He draws water from the outside tap and places the battered steel pan over the naked camping gas flame. Would he ever see her again? Would he want to see her again? It didn't take a genius to recognise someone who had gone over to the hard stuff – cocaine, heroin. Last night's trip was probably a gentle stroll in the park for Magda. It's a shame but she's out of reach now.

Spiked on a thorn of the yellow bouquet his eye falls on a couple of two-inch squares of blotting paper. A thick black symbol is crudely stamped off centre, the ink bleeding into the thin and fibrous paper. A Cyrillic letter of the alphabet? A gift from Bulgaria, perhaps? Seb smiles in gratitude. One last trip and then he will kick it for good. Get on with repairing the house, fulfilling his promise to Nigel, and get his life in order.

The day passes slowly. He spends the day writing lists of jobs and items needed. He will cash his Giro in the village tomorrow and begin the long process of making the house habitable again.

There is little point starting anything today. Seb layers himself in warm clothes in defence against the penetrating draughts whistling under the rotten doors and window frames. He lies on the sofa, pulling cushions on top of his shrinking body. From the cuff of his gloves he pulls out the two squares Magda left him and places them both under his tongue. Although the joy is likely to be much diminished after last night's trip, he may as well surrender one last time.

Within seconds Seb feels his heart slow to the rhythm of a tolling bell. What is happening? Where is that childlike happiness that usually builds and builds to a towering, bubbling euphoria? The demons are out for him tonight. He should scrabble, hide, dig deep down into the earth. Hide? But his hands aren't his own. Something is sitting on his chest. Squeezing his heart dry. Sucking out his breath. The demons are taking his strength. His vitality. Vital. Vitals. He clutches his stomach to press down on the rising nausea. But he's not there. His hands, cold, clammy, sink straight through his ribs, his offal, to the gaudy, dirty cushions beneath him. Where is he? What is happening, babe? He is become reptile. A blue reptile. A bad bad blue tripping reptile. Sleep. Anger. Sleep. Sleep. Black. Silence. Black. Black…

137

Chapter 18

December 1978

Sorcha
The Academy, Liverpool

Sorcha chooses her clothes with care. An old pair of denims from the back of the wardrobe still fit or are even slightly too loose. She weighs less now after the two children than before she was married. From a Cornish holiday, a fisherman's smock, stiff but suitably artisanal. She backcombs her hair, fastening a black velvet bow at the back and applies a brief spritz of *Ma Griffe* before leaving the house to board the train for the city centre.

She emerges from the underground into a shadowy street. Barriers weighted down with wet sandbags stop her crossing the road into the path of a noisy demonstration. As a thickly corded body, the marchers fill the street, leaders banging drums slung round their necks. Their faces look so young, tilted up into the cool air of the street, filling the narrow space with their voices. The sharp, insistent rhythm of the drums underpins the demonstrators' chants. Now and then, a whistle or a klaxon pierce the thick sound.

She looks round for a policeman before stepping back into the protection of the underground station to watch the demo pass. "Bloody students," someone shouts from inside the tiled concourse. "Get a proper job," the man behind her shouts into the crowd. Two or three of the marchers casually flick two fingers into the air as they march by. "Fuck off yourselves," comes a shout from somewhere else inside the station. She flinches at the aggression and imagines being pushed under the feet of this moving leviathan. She slips to the back of the waiting crowd where there is more room. Warm, stale air moves up with the escalator. A greasy dust lies along the tops of tiles, cigarette machines, the ticket sellers' windows; a choking, fine-powdered steel mixes with the sweat of engines. On the opposite wall, a drunk swipes his back along the glazed tiles, swaying and singing, his surprisingly mellow baritone rolling along the low ceiling towards her.

Suddenly the procession is gone and the waiting crowd moves out into the nearly vacant street, pushing between gaps in the barriers, individuals moving rapidly between the straggling protesters pushing buggies and holding placards.

Cool, fresh air billows in. She can breathe again. These days the city is criss-crossed by protests, crush barriers and bollards. Maybe one day, the head will swallow the tail.

A few dried leaves blow across the mosaic floor as she pushes hard against the heavy front door of the Academy. Beyond the self-assured Victorian style of the entrance hall, the mood changes. Coloured flyers pinned to the notice boards rise up as she passes, calling on the proletariat to seize the means of production, to unite against racism, reclaim the streets.

Where does she fit in here? A middle-aged, privileged housewife with two children, Olivia – a lumpen, overweight fifteen-year-old and Toby, her incendiary son. What can *she* do for Ethiopia, for nuclear disarmament, for equality?

The corridor leads into a common space set out with low vinyl chairs. On the back wall, an exquisite hand-painted mural – surely a relic from the mercantile past of this building. A papier maché rhinoceros charges out into the room from a mulberry arbour, A N A R C H Y spelled out in dripping red paint across the pastoral scene. It's a crying shame.

"Sorry I'm late." She grabs a clay-stiffened apron from the hooks by the door to the studio and weaves her way to an unused wheel. Several students are already pounding and tapping blocks of wet dark clay on a heavy bench. Russell approaches her. His feet are bare, as usual, exposing long horny nails. She imagines them tearing the crisp cotton sheets of her bed, leaving traces of the street on the white threads. She needs to explain why she is late. "Got caught up the wrong side of the street from a demo. Couldn't get across. Ban the Bomb, that sort of thing." But he doesn't seem interested. Russell has one of those anti-nuclear trident badges pinned to his T-shirt. She will have to watch her words.

Russell is giving her instructions. She will have to catch up; the others are ahead of her now. She glances around the studio that occupies the entire second floor. Strip lights hang on chains from metal rafters, the one above her head buzzing intermittently. Only in summer or when the kilns are being fired is the studio warm. The rest of the time, the cold of the Mersey steals in through the peeling, metal windows, taller than two men. She shivers. Russell looks at her as if she has just expressed his own deep desire. She moves slightly away from him.

"Do you know where you are up to?" She nods. "Well, carry on. Ask me anything if you need to." He goes back to listening to a football match on a little transistor radio, exclaiming loudly at intervals. She makes her way to the corner to collect last week's work, touching Olembu lightly on his arm as she passes. He looks briefly, smilingly, over his shoulder; his dark hands guiding a spinning lump of clay glisten in the grey liquid run-off.

John had suggested a table lamp when she had asked him what she should make. She'd had a few attempts, none of them really that good. Her unfired blanks are stored under tightly tied thick plastic sheeting. She will make a decision later on the best one.

She loves the smell of the studio – less so when the kilns are firing and loading the air with acrid particles – but today the kiln is clicking and cooling and only the subterranean, musty smell of clay fills her nose. She sits for a moment deciding how to fill the afternoon. She might try some relief work and looks for a small gouger.

A bell rings almost as the football match on the radio finishes. Nearly three hours have passed. Russell stands up and claps his hands. With reluctance, she puts down the bevelling tool and, rubbing her neck, looks round the rest of the class. She feels utterly still, calm, happy.

The thought of going home is wearisome. What would it be like to be locked in this building overnight? She imagines some of the grotesque, articulated artworks, products of outlandish, febrile, adolescent imaginations coming to life, their bandages trailing, dripping plaster of Paris. Maybe this is all a bit too close to her own dreamscape – familiar but nonetheless frightening territory.

A press of students, boom town rats, rushes down the corridor. She flattens herself to the dimpled glass partition to the photography room, apologising for getting in the way.

"Watch out!" a lad in black drainpipes and American baseball jacket shouts to his near companion, pulling him exaggeratedly out of Sorcha's path. They smile at her although she feels the smile pass straight through her. What do they see, if anything at all? What is she doing here? It all feels so wrong. Dangerous. Brooding. Experimental.

She pushes open the heavy door out onto the portico, passes the fluted columns and sits on the shallow steps leading down to street level.

What frightens her more? Her own sense of dislocation? Or the thought that Olivia could, in a few short years, be part of this crowd?

The winter sunshine is warming, enlivening the colours and the smells from the street. She smells tobacco smoke.

"Sorry."

Someone is speaking to her. A man sitting a few feet and a few steps forward of her. He has turned his face to her, his eyes on her. She leans towards him to catch the words from his mouth before the gusts of city air scatter them.

"Sorry." He flourishes his half-smoked cigarette in apology. "The smoke."

"Oh, it's OK." Although she hadn't been aware until he apologised, watching the thin grey smoke twist perniciously and persistently in her direction, she feels it is only polite to now quell the urgent need to cough. "It's quite alright." Her voice sounds too bright with anxiety.

"You studying here?" He gestures inside with his thumb, ash sprinkling.

"Yes. Just started pottery classes. Only part-time. Once a week."

He nods. "Cool."

Pigeons are promenading around the square, a petrochemical sheen to their feathers. It seems entirely up to her whether the discussion continues or not. He smokes, pulling on strands of his auburn beard, nonchalant.

"What about you?"

He draws on his cigarette before answering. "Part-time tutor. Fine art." She nods. He rises quickly, grinding the cigarette stub beneath his black biker boots. She, evidently, offers little to hold his attention. Just another housewife on the path to ruin. He holds out his hand to her.

"My name's Paul. Enjoy your course. I'll see you around." He moves fluidly up the steps towards the main entrance and is gone. It is the smallest and briefest of encounters. In her empty, sparsely populated world, the brief conversation holds a significance far beyond a simple exchange of names and functions.

For, here, no one can see her dresser drawer stuffed with brown plastic pill bottles from the surgery, smell the pharmaceutical odour that lingers in that part of the bedroom. No one can see the care with which John scrutinises her every night after surgery, looking for what her face might betray about the day. He loves her, of that she is sure. He loves her dutifully. And when her spirit is up, so is his.

He can match her, blow for blow. He had found her once at the dressing table piling her hair on her head, securing it with grips, holding her breath tight and hard the better to bulge out the veins in her neck. He had squeezed her wrist until she dropped the blade, pulling her onto the floor with him, rocking and sobbing into her neck. As dawn crept by the window, he had tenderly removed all the grips from her hair and brushed it until it was sleek. That was the night she finally told him about Patrick.

He so wanted to fix her, to reach into her mind to dislodge the image of the burning airman, to drug her into placidity, drug her into loving him. She loves her medicine man.

The following week, on the last day of term, the lift doors open onto the ground floor. She holds them while the man she met on the steps – Paul – manhandles a huge canvas out into the lobby.

"Thanks."

"No problem. Do you want a hand with that?"

"Well, if you wouldn't mind. Someone's supposed to be giving me a lift. Just need to get it outside."

"I'll help you." The canvas is wrapped in newspaper and plastic sheeting. Together they shuffle it through the service area of the building and out of the fire doors to a concrete area at the back. "Is this one of yours?"

"Yes. Part of a commission for the Liverpool Assurance, eventually. Six panels of eight by six feet. Liverpool through the ages, that sort of a thing. Work in progress."

"Sounds really interesting. Any chance of being able to see it?"

"It won't be ready for a long time yet. But there's going to be a reception here at the Academy next month. Come! Do! Ah, here's my lift." A black van reverses into the compound. "I mean it. Come along. Bring…someone…anyone…people!"

Chapter 19

February 1979

Sorcha
The Academy, Liverpool

A few weeks after the exhibition, in the new term, Paul catches up with her in the car park on the wasteland opposite the Academy. There is a biting edge to the wind, blowing in straight off the river. Sorcha is cold, extremely cold, having forgotten her coat. "It was good of you to come to the exhibition. What did you think?"

"I…we…thought it was very good. Yes, very good." In truth, John had found more to appreciate than she had supposed. He'd been surprisingly easy to persuade to attend and had argued for bringing Olivia. She had guided them both, that evening, through the Academy and down the concrete steps to the Royden Gallery in the basement. Two theatre style doors were pinned open, the interior almost completely, dangerously black. A powerful disco beat vibrated her sternum.

A cheer went up as, one by one, overhead lights started to flicker and spotlights blinked themselves on. The area was partitioned into smaller, white spaces.

"Sorcha! Over here!" Paul had been standing in his own booth, six small paintings running at shoulder height along the back wall. Opposite him, a morose young man, sitting on a camping stool, head bowed low, long greasy hair hanging to the ground, arms crossed at the wrist, cigarette smouldering between his fingers, beneath a vast abstract canvas.

"Good of you to come." Paul kissed her, surprisingly, once on each cheek.

His paintings were small geological studies hanging in a row. They appeared identical, except for a change in angle here or a change in light there. She recognised them as the tumbled yellow boulders of Thurstaston Beach, the colours charged with energy, each somehow separated out yet melded together. The paintings were too delicate and precise for that loud, experimental place. A large panel leant against a side wall.

Paul stood at her shoulder as she peered into the pictures. "What do you think?" John and Olivia were in the opposite booth staring, like father like daughter, at the enormous, paint-splattered, chaotic canvas, both with their hands clenched behind their backs.

"Not sure this is quite the right place for you."

"You never know, I might sell a piece or two. Could do with some cash, goodness knows. And space. There's too many pieces stacking up behind the furniture." She covered her handbag with her hand, wanting to offer him money. After all, he had – was it, five or six children? The eldest was probably Olivia's age. He was describing to her rigging up a sort of platform in the living room from scavenged scaffolding poles, the children scampering around underneath – an uneasy alliance of creativity and childcare. "Accomplish neither very satisfactorily." He hadn't said anything about who normally looked after the children.

Olivia sipped orange juice from a stippled bottle with a straw. John balanced a tumbler on a paper plate of canapes to which his daughter and wife helped themselves, listening to a speech by the Vice Chancellor. A round of applause introduced Paul to the stage. "This is him," whispered Sorcha.

"Every inch the impoverished artist," muttered John, taking in his ill-fitting trousers, soft shirt and curious tie.

"Sssh, Dad."

The microphone shrieked and cut dead. "There's a mercy," said John. Olivia nudged him with her elbow, spilling his wine.

"Oh, Ollie. Don't be so clumsy," sighed Sorcha.

"It's alright. No harm done."

"All a bit odd, if you ask me," John had offered on the way home. Well, I'm not asking. She bit back the comment. "But I liked the bigger canvas on the floor, that section of Liverpool of his. It's got that punchy, fuck you kind of quality about it."

"Darling. Olivia's in the back."

"Olivia doesn't mind, do you Olli?" The child smirked, enjoying a triumphal alliance against her mother.

"John liked the larger canvas particularly," she offers to Paul, hating herself for appearing so anodyne and trivial. "Which is unusual since he prefers his art Dutch, maritime and nineteenth century." There is a costly van de Cappelle above the fireplace in the dining room. Would Paul know the artist? Isn't she merely throwing trinkets into the chasm between them? "He thought there was a certain, well, damn you element to the painting." A blush spreads to her chest, conscious of nearly repeating John's profanity.

"Hey, that's interesting. Never quite thought of it that way. But Scousers do have that insular, turned-in sort of attitude, I find. Despite the city being a port since God knows when. 'This is the way we do it here'," he mimed, moving his head from side to side, as if squaring up for a fight.

"Don't you like Liverpool then?"

"Not particularly. I'm a soft Southerner. Come from Dorset. Fetched up here like a bit of jetsam. What about you?"

"Yes, I like the place. But then, maybe, my city is not your city."

"What did your daughter think of it? Did she like it?"

It occurs to Sorcha that she doesn't really know Olivia's opinion. "Oh, yes, I think she liked it well enough."

They are walking across the rough ground of the car park. Two gulls are squabbling over a single cold chip despite several others disgorging from greasy white paper nearby. Empty cans skitter and roll in the breeze, like chattering monkeys. A bright yellow car with painted flames and pointed fins drives past at speed, the passenger holding a vast ghetto blaster in the open window, the jarring beat competing with the overstretched engine. As they wait to cross the road, the air fills with the smell of burning oil.

Paul turns to face her, his jacket flapping as if reflecting some inner agitation. "Actually. I wonder if I could ask an enormous favour."

She glances over his shoulder. The sun flashes hey presto from behind a bulbous grey and white cloud and its rays hit the copper windows of the insurance building. Tears fill her eyes and her hair whips around her face. "Sure," before giving herself pause to reflect.

He starts to speak as the yellow car, having circulated the patch of waste ground, crests the hill at speed. It takes off and lands skidding and bouncing, the occupants shouting and whooping and punching the air. They both step back from the edge of the pavement. She is gratified that he puts a protective arm out. "Let's go in and talk." He takes her elbow and ushers her across the road.

Once inside the lobby, she gratefully puts down her heavy bags and makes an attempt to straighten her hair. Paul is talking to her. As she has a car and has been so kind to show an interest in his work, maybe he could prevail upon her good nature to help him transport another canvas. He does not have the air of a supplicant, rather of inviting her to join him on an adventure. He speaks slowly, each word weighed and measured before given utterance. Confident, without an ounce of arrogance.

The hands of the clock above the main staircase tick over to quarter past. She will be horribly late for her class but is unable to interrupt. Nor does he ask if she has somewhere else she should be.

"I rent a space in a disused warehouse down by the Bankhall Road. I can come and go as I please and not have to paint glancing over my shoulder as I do at the Academy when working on commissions. It's very rundown like so many buildings along the dockside but there's a group of us, all doing our own work, so quite companionable."

She waits patiently for him to get to the point. She can't really ask him to hurry up.

"So, my friend's van has broken down. Or at least she got it wedged in a multi storey car park and blew the transmission. It's currently mouldering in a service bay waiting for someone to tow it away." She remembers the black van arriving for Paul at the end of the previous term.

He grins, so she grins too.

"Anyway. I know it's impossibly impudent of me to ask…" He looks out to the car park as if measuring up the Bristol.

"No, go on."

"Might I ask you to help lug another canvas across town?"

"Er, yes, I suppose so. When?"

149

"Tomorrow afternoon?"

"Er…"

"Great. You really are most kind. Must dash. Late for my class." He runs up the wide staircase away from her.

That evening she sits in a pool of lamplight, crochet on her knee. John switches on the television, returning to his armchair, hitching his trouser legs as he sits. Olivia is clumping about upstairs. What is that girl doing? Tommy Cooper is on TV, working his way ineptly through a comedy routine. Should she tell John about tomorrow's mission? John slaps his knee in helpless amusement. It annoys her that he should find these predictable, inane routines so amusing. Would he object to her helping Paul out? Does he have any grounds to object? His laughter grows louder, feels like a mockery. The comedian laughs too. She sighs and readjusts her legs under her. John glances briefly in her direction, unseeing. Why does he insist on watching this rubbish? Olivia appears at the doorway in her pyjamas.

"Oli. Come and watch." She sits alongside her father on the arm of his chair and shakes a bottle of nail varnish.

"Olivia. Don't paint your nails in here. You'll get nail varnish on the upholstery." Pointedly Olivia puts the colour on the coffee table, sidling closer to her father, who pats her shoulder. She saw it, that chummy, never-mind-girl, little pat. They guffaw together.

The room is suddenly airless. The gas fire hisses and bubbles as if it has exhausted all the available oxygen. The mass of crochet in her lap, millions and millions of minute stitches, years of work, is tangling her legs, suffocating her, dragging her down like a fishing net. Her husband and her daughter are melding into one, a crazy, mutant, jerky, barking creature. She presses her hand hard down on her chest to force air into her lungs. Her lungs, too sticky, might never inflate again. Her heart pounds to the beat from the yellow car. Tension and panic lift her out of her chair.

"Daddy!" She hears Olivia's voice. "Mummy's…"

"Alright darling. Nothing to worry about. You go upstairs."

"Aw, do I have to? I like this programme."

"Yes. For the best. Night, darling."

"Night, Dad." Olivia kisses him and leaves the room. She does not say goodnight to her mother. Sorcha flaps and gulps for air. That hideous man has gone from the screen. John is by her chair, stroking her hand, his back to the television set.

"Deep breaths. Deep breaths. There we go. There we go." Why does he have to repeat everything? "Nice and calm now." He waits, staring into her face, kneeling on the floor. He counts backwards, slowly, from ten. "And when I get to one, you will be feeling a lot calmer and in control." She nods. "Three. Two. One." A tiny bulge of air is admitted into her lungs. Her heart centres itself in her chest again. Her legs stop their dance. "Glass of water?" She nods. "And a pill?"

"Yes please."

Chapter 20

February 1979

Sorcha
Bankhall Street, Liverpool

She drives through parts of the city she has never visited. Paul points the way through the windscreen, directing her through acres of wasteland. Three once graceful Georgian houses stand together, either end of the terrace blasted or fallen away, bricks discarded for yards around. Each window has been broken, as if the press of years of neglect has burst through and shattered the glass. Stone steps rise up to metal mesh doorways, incongruously topped by elaborate but peeling fanlights. Green mould runs down the stuccoed façade behind loose drainpipes. River mist softens and obscures the clusters of high rise blocks – a new world trampling over the old. As they turn towards the Dock Road, even the pubs and boarding houses have a grandiose air about them, their ornate scrollwork and moulded terracotta made grotesque by decay. It is a strange landscape, she thinks, where shame and corruption scuttle like rats. How could the city have become like this?

"Turn right here." Paul takes them between parallel terraces of small houses, the muddy-red brickwork flat, functional. She might have expected more signs of life but each door is closed, nets drawn across the windows.

"It's all a bit eerie," she wants to say but holds back from showing any discomfort. This is probably Paul's world. She presses the door lock down discretely with her elbow and her foot to the accelerator.

"So tell me about yourself. All I know is that you like pottery. And nice cars." Paul eyes the walnut glovebox and olive coloured leatherwork.

"Oh, this is my husband's car. I just borrow it sometimes on college days." Roadside hazard lights flash and she stops to let a fast-moving stream of trucks swing through vast dock gates onto the road. A handful of women in headscarves shake their fists and shout abuse at the drivers. She turns to look at Paul, puzzled.

"Polish coal. The women are in support of the miners. The government is going to close down the mines so we can buy our coal cheaper elsewhere."

"Oh." Progress, she supposes, but shame for the families. Families everywhere in the North – Yorkshire, Lancashire, Merseyside.

"Can't fight the inevitable, I suppose." Paul says. He glances at the shouting women and smiles. One of them tells him to fuck off.

"You're in the wrong car."

"Yes." He laughs with gusto and she is suddenly warmed by his good humour.

The final truck pulls away and the women sit back down on their garden chairs. "So, go on. Tell me about yourself."

"Not much to say, really. Married. John's a GP. Two children, Olivia and Toby. Toby's at boarding school. Olivia lives at home with us, goes to the local girls' school."

"So, a good life, then you'd say?"

"Yes. On the whole."

"And what brought you to the Academy? It's got a bit of a reputation as a hotbed of radicals and anarchists. Wouldn't have thought it was quite your environment."

"No. But I didn't know that when I applied. Not sure how easy it is to make a political statement out of a lump of clay, anyway!"

Again, that warming laugh. "Unless you throw it through a window or at a visiting politician."

"Must work on my overarm."

They are passing yards and yards of high brick wall, surmounted by coils of barbed wire. From time to time, the car wheels fall into disused tram tracks and the vehicle shudders and bucks. She pulls hard on the large steering wheel to get it back on the cobbles covered by thin, worn asphalt. Beyond the towering walls, a sentry of cranes. They remind her of the rows of poplar trees she'd seen in France, planted on the birth of a daughter as a future dowry. Glimpsed through the succession of dock gates, rusting locos and chequerboards of cars waiting for export. Gulls wheel above.

"We need to turn right here." She noses the car down a street lined with chain-link fencing and furniture and tyre outlets. "Over the canal bridge. This is us. Park here."

She parks in the shade of a tall, Victorian, brick-built warehouse. The bricks are old, slender, friable, dotted with lime and pebbles. She wonders where they were made. She feels a kinship with the brick workers, fashioning clay. Surely clay serves best as a monument, not a tool for protest.

The building has a monumental beauty about it, rising squarely from the canal-side, three storeys of long paned windows beneath dog-tooth detail in black brick. Slender wooden doors, one above the other, open directly out of the blank wall beneath a redundant hoist. She follows Paul off the street into a large open space. In the centre is an enormous tumble of oily black cogs and wheels, gears, rods and shafts. Is this deliberate art or abandoned junk? She's really not sure. Light is shining in from all four sides.

Footsteps resonate above her head on wooden floorboards. An occasional knot hole allows a glimpse to the floor above. A thin column of sunshine runs obliquely through one such hole, within which dances warm dust. The lines between the floorboards run straight, blackened with tar. Muffled music arrives from somewhere as well as the sound of hammering and knocking. But for the music, these could be the sounds of the last hundred years within the industrial cavity of this building.

"Come with me." Paul races up a flight of wooden stairs behind a curved brick wall. "My space is on the first floor." She climbs cautiously to the next floor which mirrors the one below except there is even more light. Dust dances around Paul's heels as he marches to one corner. A scaffolding tower rises from a cluster of trestle tables, each crowded with tubes of paint, brushes, knives, palette knives, pens, rock samples, photographs, jars. She walks past a group of garishly clad mannequins, bolts of cloth leaning against the wall, a long cheval mirror. "I share this space with Madeleine. She does installations and theatre design." A different world.

Madeleine's mannequins have a Bowie-esque quality to them, androgynous, pale as moonlight, undernourished. At their feet or pinned about their frames are miniature replicas of themselves. She wonders if these might be boudoir dolls – haunting, mocking alter egos, talismans of the greater self, gifts to admirers and followers. Or just weird little suckers.

Wasn't it only the slightly mad scions of the wealthy and privileged who are encouraged to get creative with bits of fabric and wire? Certainly the Sunday supplements seem to suggest so.

Unless Madeleine belonged to the French aristocracy, then art has democratised itself, shifted, like so much of society.

Sorcha knows she can't possibly ask but is curious how Paul makes a living. Does he earn enough to feed himself and his family? Looking at him, his contoured cheeks, knotted hands, frayed jacket; maybe meals aren't that regular. She suddenly thinks of tonight's supper – clams, spaghetti, lemon juice, freshly chopped parsley, chilled Sauvignon – food for the paysanne (John liked to eat simply) but probably a mockery to such as Paul. She makes her way to the canal-side window, noting as she passes the scrumpled confectionery and pasty wrappers. Would she – truly – sacrifice all the wealth she had for a creative life?

As if reading her mind, Paul observes, "You could get a space here. Dirt cheap. Nobody knows what to do with these warehouses anymore now the port's in decline. You know, if you wanted to take up pottery as more than just a hobby. It's dry, safe. A good place to work."

She looks out of the window, onto the canal. The water is brown, sludgy, yet the reflections dancing on the ceiling are white and pure. "I don't think I've quite got what it takes. You know, no real axe to grind. Lampshades and tankards – that's about the long and short of it for me." Paul shrugs but doesn't argue, turning his attention instead to a large canvas in the corner.

"This is the next section. Don't look too closely. It won't mean much out of context. Wait till you see it all in one piece. Give me a few minutes, I'll just wrap it up in something. Sit down." She sits on the split vinyl car seat that he clears for her. It is low and rocks uncertainly on its metal frame. She positions her hands awkwardly on her knees.

Crazy to think of her pottery as art but yet undoubtedly it did come from some creative impulse. Maybe if she did take up some studio space in this warehouse, the environment would confer some artistic credibility on her work. Becalm her. Re-centre her. Although what she had to protest about, she didn't really know.

Paul had told her not to look at his canvas but she can't resist looking at it leaning against the end of the trestle while he rummages around looking for wrapping. A kaleidoscope of bright colours, seemingly spilled, random, yet if she twists her head she might just see a pattern emerge as the colours graduate, flow. She can just make out a square church spire, possibly the radio tower, cranes.

It takes a long time for Paul to wrap the canvas. He is slow, meticulous, unhurried and time is fast moving to when she needs to be home and see to her domestic duties.

"Paul."

"Yes. Be with you in just a few moments."

Why hadn't she told John of her mission today? She had had opportunity. Surely he would not object. Maybe he would be *too* encouraging, *too* happy to see her branching out. Perversely, his pleasure would undermine her pleasure. If she had told him that she was skipping college today to help a lecturer transport a section of his work from an atelier across town, he would have smiled broadly and been glad that she was getting out more. And that would have ruined the entire thing.

"Finished now. Sorry to keep you waiting."

"I'll hold the doors for you."

At the car, they realise they have no means of attaching the painting.

"Thought you might have a roof rack or something."

"Er, no. John would think that was like…"

"Ropes?" She shakes her head. "Well, we'll just have to hold it on and drive slowly."

"Are you joking? What if it falls off or gets damaged?"

"It won't. I've got confidence in your driving."

"Are you absolutely sure? It seems a huge risk. Surely somewhere around here we can get some rope?"

"No. No time. And, anyway, you need to get home. I saw you look at your watch at least twenty times."

"OK," she agrees reluctantly.

Paul hauls the canvas on top of the car. It covers the entire roof and overhangs the front, casting a shadow on the windscreen. "Wind your window down and just hold on."

"What about the steering and the handbrake and all that?" Her voice is rising with anxiety. God, please please please don't have an episode just now. She checks herself. It's not anxiety; it's excitement.

"You'll be alright. I'll change gear."

"You're crazy."

"You're just as crazy."

She drives at twenty miles an hour through the city, pulling awkwardly at the steering wheel with her left hand. School girls giggle behind their hands, someone at the dock gates swings a football rattle, a bus driver adjusts his mirror to take a better look while the passengers passively stare down at them. Paul murmurs encouragement and directions. She snaps at him, "Be careful," when he mistakes second gear for fourth.

"Sorry. Never driven a car before."

"Seriously!" She stares at him in astonishment.

"Lights are green."

"I know! I know!"

He recoils at the sharpness of her tone. She might apologise but feels the balance of culpability lies firmly with Paul for involving her in such a reckless enterprise. In a moment of horror, she imagines the canvas slipping from their grasp and cartwheeling into a pedestrian or across another car's windscreen. What if her grip on the wheel slipped and she steered them disastrously off course? What if one of John's patients saw them?

The car begins its slow ascent of the concrete flyover above the city. She grips even tighter to the wheel and to the canvas, staring fixedly ahead, steeling herself for imminent disaster.

"You need to get over into the right-hand lane."

"Well, bloody indicate then!"

"Alright." Paul's temper is getting as short as hers but she does not care. A motorbike swerves round them at speed and crosses in front. She wants to hold the horn down hard but can't.

"We're nearly there."

"Thank Christ."

She parks at the Academy steps and slowly unpicks her stiffened fingers and releases the canvas. "You can go now, if you need to."

"Right. I will." She hurries home.

Chapter 21

July 1980

Sorcha
St Luke's, Liverpool

She knows of St Luke's. The whole city knows St Luke's – the Bombed-out Church – on Leece Street. Hit during the Blitz of 1941. May, the month that killed fifteen hundred citizens. A thousand seriously wounded. Standing today, no roof, no altar, no pulpit, no organ, yet still utterly holy. A building of contradictions. A monument to the Liverpool dead. Celebrating the life of the city today. "Like an Ark," Paul described it. Sorcha walks to the church from Lime Street Station. Paul had invited her to view the painting being assembled for its first public viewing at a Peace Fair before being installed behind the copper windows of the insurance offices next to the Academy.

"What are you going to call the painting?" she'd asked.

"Not too sure, actually. The company wanted the city rising out of the ashes. Thirty-five years after the end of the war. Renewal. That sort of thing."

"*Resurgam ex igne.*"

"Undoubtedly."

The shadows cast on the turf are dark yet pierced by sunlight through the arched windows. She looks up as she approaches and sees the few jagged panes of glass still caught fast in the stone-fretted windows.

A series of booths beneath stretched yacht canvas line both sides of the inner space. A rudimentary path runs through the middle, the grass on either side trodden and muddy. The air smells of rain and hot wires. She can see Paul, rope tied round his waist, awkwardly climbing up a scaffolding tower. She lingers on her way over to see him, picking up polished gem stones, pewter, turned wood, second-hand records. He calls to her over the heads of everyone. "What do you think?"

The piece is vast, stretching up into the space before the empty bell tower. Central to the work, a high arching Church window assembled in splashes of colour, as if all the natural elements of the city, from the mud of the Mersey, bricks, limestone, park flowers, leaves from the plane trees, exhaust, mist, metal, humanity, blood had been splattered onto and teased out of the stone. Haphazardly, out of true and out of scale, a tumble of buildings falls from top to bottom. A trail of verdigris, like a lightning conductor, sections the piece, while fires burn, suns and moons and planets spin, shadows criss-cross. The effect is mesmerising, awesome. "Do you like it?" She shakes her head, not knowing what to say. "No?"

It seems too awkward to be scrutinising this man's canvas, as if he had been eviscerated in front of a crowd. Suddenly she can see it – the city as an opened cadaver. Shards of bone, rivers of blood, yellow sinew, the clear blue of a vein all chopped and mingled into a rising cityscape.

"They're putting out a few chairs. Why not have a seat and have a good look and then tell me what you really think? I've got a few things to finish off and then you can buy me lunch," he shouts down over the head of the young man tethered to the end of Paul's rope.

She's glad he's asked for lunch, which she will happily supply.

She sits in front of the towering canvas. It feels strange to seek peace and contemplation amongst the noise and traffic of the city. The sun is warm about her shoulders, her back turned to the hurly-burly within the church space.

She recalls the only time she'd seen him eat – when Madeleine had brought in chips and a bottle of cheap German wine to the studio they shared. Madeleine had made a perfunctory offer to share with Sorcha, clearly hoping that she'd refuse – which she did. Paul, on the other hand, had carefully squared a piece of the greasy wrapping paper and watched hungrily as Madeleine tipped the steaming chips onto his rudimentary plate. He'd rinsed a plastic wine glass in the small, paint-spattered sink and held it out for Madeleine to pour. From the low car seat, she'd watched him consider each mouthful, clearly enjoying the hot salty taste of the chips and the sweetness of the wine.

Maybe this is what makes him an artist. A minute consideration of every detail, a thankfulness as well as an unchallengeable conviction in the rightness of his purpose as an artist.

Again, Sorcha wonders whether she could commit herself to a life of hunger assuaged only by sporadic offers of food and money in exchange for creative brilliance. Unlikely. Her ambition only reaches as far as the rough-cut, rudimentary stoneware items shaped by her hands.

Her eyes flicker again over the painting. It draws her in. There is so much detail. It feels like plunging down a rabbit hole.

The subject is clearly Liverpool. She can make out the familiar landmarks bizarrely juxtaposed. There is the elegant Cunard Building, the Bluecoat Chambers, the ruddy hues of the

Anglican Cathedral, the Rotunda Theatre, St Luke's itself; even, she smiles when she recognises it, the warehouse in Bankhall Road. Many of the buildings are smudged, abstract; others are depicted in fine architectural detail. Along the choppy blue waters of the Mersey, coracles and clippers and ocean-going liners form a flotilla and mingle amongst mythical sea creatures.

Every element makes sense yet floats freely, the background disengaged from the foreground. There is a momentum and a movement to the painting. Idly her eyes follow a V-shaped formation of swans flying below her, between her vantage point in the sky and a chequered, lineated cityscape beneath. Clouds billow. She has seen these clouds before, massing between the darkening horizon and the darkening sea to bring in the coming night.

The clouds change, turning from rose-tinted white to mechanical grey, their form no longer becalmed but on the move, smearing as if the globe beneath them is spinning out of control. The swans merge. The feathers across their strong backs flatten and smooth over. They lose their cloud-like sheen and turn grey, like rolled steel.

Bombs are falling on the city. A ship in dock explodes, its name in golden letters firing off in all directions M.A.L.A.K.A.N.D. Red flashes mark the path of incendiary bombs. But, wait! There is more disaster.

Disaster in the sky. An airman scrabbles at the canopy of his plane. He is shouting. Helpless. He is shouting her name, Sorcha! Sorcha! The burning mass is about to hit the ground. She is shouting his name. Patrick! Patrick!

She is lying on the charred ground. Voices around her. Her own mouth is dry, her lips sealed together. Only her throat moves, painfully. 'Patrick'.

The light changes as the voices quieten and someone moves in towards her, a head lowering to hers. 'Darling?'

Patrick?

Her body aches. She reaches out her hand. Can she – just once, just one more time – place her hand against his smooth-shaven cheek? Place a finger along his bottom lip, inviting him to bite down on her knuckle? Look deep into his storm-tossed eyes? Hold him close through his 'megrims'? Pour him another drink and hold his hand steady as he brings the glass to his mouth? Pin his flailing arms to the bed they shared?

Something deep is telling her that is all impossible now.

"Darling? Can you hear me? You're safe now. You're home."

It's not ash she's lying in. It's her own bed. The light is dim. Voices out in the corridor brightly saying that Mrs Munro will be alright and to carry on with your work, Aya.

She lies still and listens to the voices. There are two in the room with her, figures bent over opposite sides of the bed.

John – as usual. And…and…Paul? How can that be? They are talking quietly, murmuring as if what they are saying she should not be privy to. She listens intently behind closed eyes.

"I can't thank you enough for bringing Sorcha home and calling me."

How did Paul know where to bring her? She had always been very careful not to give any hints about where she lived, thinking she already gave away too much with her colonial vowels, quality clothes and bespoke car.

"I thought it better to bring her home. You always say, you know what Sorcha needs when she has an episode like this."

Always say? A fog chases through Sorcha's brain. She can't understand what is being said here.

"She'll be fine. There are times when she gets a little

'overwhelmed'." She can hear the implied apology in her husband's voice.

"Lucky I was there to help out." Paul's voice is, as usual, slow and modulated. His concern seems genuine. But concern for whom? For her? Or does he have some responsibility to John, her husband? And, if so, how has that come about? "She seemed fine. I was rigging the painting together when I looked down. She had fallen off her chair and was collapsed onto the ground. I tell you, for one moment, I was very, very concerned."

"These attacks are probably more alarming to the onlooker."

You bastard, she thinks. You utter bastard. How can you possibly say that?

"I am most terribly worried that something in the painting triggered Sorcha's episode. Although she couldn't speak properly, it was if she wanted to tell me something. She was stuttering. A name, possibly?"

"Patrick?"

"Yes, it might have been."

There is a long pause to the conversation. The light shifts as both men pull away from their bedside vigil.

"I should perhaps have been a little bit more specific when I asked you to keep an eye on my wife. Something happened when she was a young woman in Rhodesia. She was witness to a very unfortunate incident. A young airman, who was assumed to have been in love with Sorcha and, it was rumoured, having an affair with her own mother, took his life in a very dramatic way in front of her very eyes."

Sorcha lies utterly still and utterly mute on the bed while John explains the lurid facts. But what could be more vile than Paul's betrayal of their friendship? She might spring out of bed, grab Paul by the collar and shout and scratch and scream that he is supposed to be *her* friend, not a stooge of her husband's. How on earth had the two of them met? How had John inveigled his way into Paul's consciousness such that he, Paul, had been persuaded to 'keep an eye' on her?

Her heart is pounding, her chest is heaving. Paul is *her* friend. *Her* way out of this stifling house, the utter tyranny of meals on the table, being pleasant to the daily help, practice dinners, the unstopping, selfish demands of the children, the relentlessness of life. *Hers.*

Has it all been a huge set-up?

"I think we can leave her now. She seems settled. She'll sleep it off and be right as rain in the morning. Come. Let me give you something for your troubles and I'll drive you home."

"Really, I'll be fine. I'm only a bus ride away."

Competent, professional hands push their way under the mattress, tucking her in. John kisses her forehead. She wants to spit in his eye. How dare he? How dare he take what is hers, what is uniquely hers and make it his? She will never forgive him. Never. Ever.

But there is no escape.

For now she must surrender. Sleep. Let the blackness take her over.

She wakes into a softer light. Testing herself, joint by joint, limb by limb; she can move again. She twists her head on the pillow towards the window. A cup of tea has been placed on the bedside cabinet. Evening traffic is moving past outside. There is a sound of a lawnmower. John must be mowing the lawn. John. What is it that she needs to remind herself about John? She thinks hard. Wasn't there a conversation? A bus. Who's on the bus? Paul. Paul? Does he live this side of the water? He never said. Does that explain the connection between John and Paul? Is Paul one of John's patients?

But it does not matter because, by giving up Paul, she will give up John's means to control her. Decision made.

Another more unusual, more insistent connection seems to be forming in her mind. What is it that John said? Her mother?

Sorcha swings her legs out of bed with the suddenness of the shock, the awful recall of what John had told Paul. Had Grace, her mother, really truly had an affair with Patrick?

She slides off the bed and vomits onto the carpet.

"Dr Munro! Come quickly!"

Feet running. Hands, again, pulling her nightgown down to cover her cold exposed backside. Voices. "Come on, darling. Let's get you decent and back into bed."

Chapter 22

July 1998

Olivia
Dock Road, Liverpool

"Can't we go and live with Granny and Grandpa?"

"Absolutely not!"

"Why not? I could get the ferry to see Dad. Take my bike."

"No!"

"But why not? It's not fair. I'm never going to see Daddy again. Or..."

"Will you just stop your whining!" The traffic is slow moving out of the city. She throws a comic from the front seat to the back of the car. "Read that!"

They could easily take the tunnel, drive to Granny Sorcha and Grandpa John's leafy suburb, park outside, make their way up the garden path, hand-in-hand, arriving on the doorstep like two refugees. Dad would answer the door and pull her in tight for a hug, knowing from the look on her face that she needed help.

Sorcha would not come to the door. Instead she and Zac would be ushered in to sit on the overstuffed sofas while Mother finished whatever she was doing first. Daddy would make coffee and then sit, waiting for the audience to commence, for them to make a full account of themselves. He might stroke the back of her hand with a finger and grin sadly at Zac but it would not be in his gift to offer much more.

Olivia would become a supplicant before a High Priestess, stuttering to explain why, given all the privileges of a good husband who works well to provide for his family, she is leaving him. Doesn't Olivia know that money counts for a lot these days and is the very glue that holds all those disparate pieces together into some sort of arrangement that allows everybody to just get on with their lives?

Behind Mummy's eyes would be that look of exasperation she is so good at. The look that says, 'I had to crawl out of a pit of snakes to get where I am now'. She knows about Mummy's pit of snakes. Well, she'd peered over the edge at times. She knows how Mummy hated her early life in Rhodesia. How her own father, Guy, was a bully and a tyrant. How she had met Daddy while working in a hotel in Scotland. How Uncle Seb had died of an overdose. How, until Mummy went to art school to study ceramics, she had been half-crazed. She knows about Daddy's supply of secret medication. The house still rings with the sound of doors slamming, plates smashing, screams.

So, why child, the look on Mummy's face would say, why child can you not manage your own life? What disasters and demons have *you* faced compared to mine? What gives *you* the right to bring your chaos into *my* house?

But, Mummy dearest, *you* are my disaster, *you* are my demon.

And then Mummy's eyes will flicker to Zac and then back to her – to the clothes she is wearing, her midriff, her unkempt hair. Her eyes will unerringly fall on her scuffed shoes, the missing button, the broken nails.

Oh, there is no way on this earth she could withstand such scrutiny and such evident disappointment.

And poor old Daddy will be fidgeting in his chair, crossing and uncrossing his legs, telling Sorcha to hold on now, I think we are going a bit far here. We? We? And if he were to win that particular round and have Olivia and Zac to stay for a few days, far away up in the attic bedrooms of course, then he would definitely lose the battle. She just couldn't do that to him.

So, no, she won't be taking the tunnel and driving to that leafy suburb. Instead she continues along the dock road, past the once grand drinking and boarding houses, past the terminals for the big ships, past the industrial estates, security fencing and cameras, canal-side warehouses. The car tyres sing and rumble over exposed cobbles and tram tracks on their way north to the Lakes.

She looks in the rear-view mirror, regretting her harsh words to her son. "Oh my goodness, Zac. What's the matter?"

His eyes look back at her, red-rimmed, silent tears falling onto the comic crumpled on his lap. He shrugs and looks out of the window. Veering into a bus stop, Olivia stops the car and opens the back door to sit beside Zac. He stares at the brick wall.

"I'm sorry." She grips his arm. He snatches it away. "Come here."

Olivia releases his seatbelt and pulls him towards her. He doesn't resist, turning till he is across her lap, his face close to hers. She wraps her arms round his slender, bony body and rocks him backwards and forwards. His tears trickle down her neck. She presses him to her. "Hey. Hey. Hey. Everything will be alright. I promise. I promise. We'll come down and see Daddy lots. And he will come and see us too. And we'll find a nice house and we can paint your bedroom and put your posters up."

She continues to rock him and reassure him, all the while offering up a silent prayer, breathless with the enormity of it all, that she can give this tender child a safe and happy future, that he will flourish and forgive her.

Zac stops crying and moves a strand of hair from across her face.

There's a knock on the car window. "You alright, love?" A woman has detached herself from the crowd waiting for the bus and peers through the back window. Olivia nods. The woman turns and comments over her shoulder, "They're alright. Just having a grizzle." Two other shoppers bend their heads to look in through the car window.

As he climbs back into his seat, Olivia notices a red mark above his temple. The corner of the comic must have hit him when she threw it. Oh dear God.

Chapter 23

September 2000

Olivia
Cumbria

She wakes with a start to the echo of a loud noise. Had something just fallen off a shelf or a car backfired? The sound, the meaning of the sound is still somewhere inside her head. She might still catch it. Play it again. She plays it again. A sharp noise. Not just once. Repeated. There it is again. She clutches her forehead. There's pain in her temples, at the back of her eyes. The sound rings in her ears. Louder. And louder.

She slides off the sofa and, pulling her wrap round her, shuffles to the front door. "Coming." The bulky shape behind the glass adds the final flourish, the coda, to his knock.

"Delivery."

"Alright. Alright!"

She pulls the silken ties around her waist. Her wrap is too short. It seems to slip out of her grasp.

"Minute." Her voice is a desiccated croak, her mouth parched.

The light in the living room is orange, morning sun shining through the open weave curtains. She kicks an empty wine bottle, sending it scudding and twirling across the wooden floor.

It rolls to rest against the front door. She knows who it is. Harold, the curiously shaped courier, belt fastened tight into his oedema. "Can you leave it on the step? I'm not…I'm not…" He maybe can't hear her because he presses his ear to the small pane of crinkled glass in the door. His face fragments, his flesh skewing into irregular shapes bordered by the darkness of his hair. She wants to be sick.

"What's that you're saying, love?"

The letter box is only a few inches off the floor. She crawls along the floor and curls against the door frame lifting the heavy, iron shutter to whisper through the black, nylon bristles, "I'm not very well. Can you leave it on the step?"

The light in the hallway brightens. Harold pokes four chubby fingers through the letter box and waggles them. Why? Might she hold his hand – or his fingers at least – just for a second? Would he let her?

The door reverberates with his voice. His head must be against the door. "I can't. Needs to be signed for."

She quells the nausea within her. "Minute." She rises slowly, with concentration, letting the metal shutter fall behind his fast retreating fingers. Laughter bubbles up through the bile.

Harold is standing on the doorstep, his large boots, untied and unwieldy, are planted wide apart on the sleek quarry tiles. He is holding a shoe-box sized parcel. "Ms Tyler? Ms *Olivia* Tyler?"

"You know I am."

"We have to ask." He glances up from programming his black gadget. Something catches his eye. The soft dove grey silk falls a fraction from her shoulders and billows slightly. "Sign here please." She reaches her arm forward to give her signature. Her wide sleeve brushes against the back of his hand. "Thank you." He turns from her and she watches his loose bootlaces flick flack

173

up the path towards the open door of his old-fashioned people carrier. Brown boxes press against the grimy back windows. He hauls himself across the frayed fabric of the front seat and toots merrily as he drives off, waving a hand out of the window. She leans forward to pick up the milk, relishing the momentary freedom and exposure she gives her body.

"Oh Christ," she mutters. The strain of moving even slightly off the vertical triggers a rise of nausea again and she rushes to the bathroom to vomit. The stream is dark red and flows easily from her wide mouth.

They hadn't eaten last night, she remembers now. For once Neil had come round early. Her heart had leapt when she heard the van pull up on the drive. It was only six o'clock. Why so early? Were they due to go out? Had he come to make peace after their argument? Or, and the thought thumped her in the chest, had he come to collect his things?

She had counted out his passage through the house. One, two, three as he walked into the kitchen to dump his stuff. Four, five, six as he pulled a bottle of wine from the rack and poured himself a large glass. Her wine. Wine that he had not paid for. She pictured him emptying the jelly-bowl sized glass down his throat. Glug, glug, glug as he poured a refill. Seven, eight, nine as he switched the television on over the breakfast bar and pulled up a stool. American Football night. She waited for him to call out, to come looking for her. Twenty minutes passed before she went into the kitchen. "There you are," he said flatly. He didn't look at her, his arms folded, his fingers gripping and massaging his biceps.

She didn't answer but moved over to light the stove. He was obviously uncomfortable. Is this how his guilt reveals itself? Apparently he felt no corresponding kick of joy on seeing her either. In fact, she thinks he hates her. Hates her for holding him captive. Hates her because, right now, he needs her.

She imagines killing him. Right now. She imagines the hiss of a cold steel blade as it flies through the air and lodges cleanly and neatly between his shoulder blades. For the fantasy to be complete, however, he is not sitting on the bar stool in his grubby hoody but is hunched over the kitchen table, his torso naked, flesh, blood, steel. But hers is a practical mind. Could you actually throw a cleaver some distance into someone's back? Would it lodge there, or is there too much muscle and sinew? What about the ribs? She will have to research this, to make the fantasy workable.

Her favourite, and one that plays in her mind again and again and again, is the gun. As with the cleaver, the execution is accomplished in a swift, double-arching movement. She knocks him to the ground with her left fist, following the curve with the gun in her right hand. Whoosh whoosh bang. Multiple deaths. Over and over and over. Satisfaction every time.

"You're here early."

He didn't take his eyes from the screen. "Yeah." No explanation.

"I might cook. Want something to eat?"

"Not bothered thanks."

She was starving. Etiquette, worn thin over the last eleven months, still dictates to Olivia that she feeds anyone in her house around mealtimes. Even fat, loathsome, self-serving slugs. If they don't eat, she doesn't eat. More Geisha than girlfriend. She switched the gas off, leaning the heels of her hands against the stovetop. She sighed but he wasn't listening.

Eleven months! Who's counting, he might say? It's more of a girl thing, she might shrug. She can hear Scorn, his little alter ego, whisper conspiratorially in his ear, 'Hey buddy. Do you count how many times you go for a slash? Do you *count* how many times you have a…?' She gets the meaning. Counting's for losers. Counting's for people who hold on too tight. Counting's for people who don't know how to just kick back and have a good time.

How had it come to this? A one-night pick-up negotiated against the juke box in the Swan to intermittent visiting rights that brought no joy to either of them.

She brought a wine glass to the breakfast bar and sat down. "If you want a drink, you'll have to get another bottle. This one's finished." The most he'd spoken to her since getting here.

Neil carried on shouting at the TV, adding his profanities to the roar of the crowd and excitable chatter of the commentators. She was just not there. This is the consequence of stillness, tranquillity, passive resistance. You are just not there. A nobody.

What was it his mother said once? "At least he doesn't steal." Oh, but, poor deluded lady, he does.

There is a particular arrangement to his face. An appeal she can't resist. An appeal that he really doesn't deserve. A black and ugly heart should not be so beautiful. But he has stolen her heart.

Then the music came on, pulsing into the night. They had danced for a while, until a sort of moroseness descended on him.

She knows she is the wrong woman. The thought pulsed inside her head with each beat. Hendrix, Machine Gun, metal screeching on metal, sparks flying, steel bending beyond endurance. Her nail beds, her teeth throbbing, aching. Skynyrd, Saturday Night Special, unrepentant rhythm picked up by modulating guitar dulling the driving, repetitive song line. Funny how many songs had guns in them. Woosh Woosh Bang.

She vaguely recalls locking up and leaving Neil downstairs going through her record collection. In the early dawn, there he was claiming – as if *droit de seigneur* – more than half the mattress. Her half of the mattress, actually, leaving Olivia only a narrow tract to sleep in. Just another of the rearrangements and adjustments that have had to be made.

She had twisted herself up onto an elbow to look at him in the grey light. He was sleeping on his side. Balanced, poised. A long vertical line ran down his back, from the nape of his neck, between his shoulder blades, to below the bed sheets. A fold in his skin. She imagined inserting a few coins or tokens into that crease, just as builders used to into the rafters of their new house. For luck. To ward away bad luck. To appease those creatures that just want to wreck everything.

She had wanted to ride on the long, slow sweep of his sleeping breath. Slowly in. Slowly out. Slowly in. Slowly out. Lift and fall. Lift and fall. She matched her breath to his, thinking it would calm her racing heart. But it didn't work. Her heart was way too antsy.

He is beautiful. On the outside. Yes, she knows the smell of his shit in the morning.

He sighed in his sleep. One of those deep, juddering sighs that come every hundred or so breaths. His body was resetting itself, even in sleep. Not that she's paranoid or anything, but instead of a reset, that sigh began to sound like a resolution made. Or a sadness expelled. Or annoyance. What's going on in there, in his sleep-drenched mind? She'd wanted to shake him awake, just to see, in that brief millisecond before his mate Scorn woke up too, what secrets lay behind those eyes.

She heard a quiet, muffled buzz buzz. His phone having a petit mal under the pillow. Somebody wants him. She checked the time. It's twenty-three minutes past five in the feckin' morning. Who had him in their sights at 05:23 in the morning?

His phone buzzed again. He woke up, pulling the phone from under the pillow and himself out of bed in one movement.

One by one, those coins she'd placed between his shoulder blades fell silently and mockingly to the floor. So she went downstairs to find that bottle of wine.

She hiccups. Progress. No vomit.

Zac will be home, back from his Dad's in a few short hours, looking for that delivery of new trainers.

Chapter 24

September 2005

Olivia
Cumbria

There is a smell of gas in the small hallway as Olivia pushes open the swollen front door to let herself and Zac in out of the rising wind. Zac is shivering, goose pimples peppering his thin legs, bare above his football socks. Autumn leaves push their way in front of them.

"Go and get yourself out of your wet things and run a bath."

"OK, Mum." Zac scampers noisily up the steep wooden stairs on his hands and feet.

The house is cold as if, in the few hours they were at under-14s football training, it had forgotten its duty to protect and guard this small family of two. There is a combination of north wind, frosty temperature and alignment of the mischief-making stars that ensures the pilot light goes out at least once every winter. Tonight is that very night.

She looks out of the window – there does seem to be a malevolent, orangey-red planet winking down directly on high; the wind is banging the outhouse door like an unmedicated child. She presses the reset button. The sounds of the boiler firing into life are punctuated by the dull thunk of Zac's wet gear falling to the tiles of the hallway floor. "There you are, Mum," he calls from the top landing.

"Thanks," she shouts back, ironically.

"'S'alright," Zac answers, unaware of any sarcasm.

"Just check the water's hot enough and have a quick bath. Come down when you're finished for supper." The bathroom door closes.

She switches on the television above the breakfast bar. The sound is off but the images of cadets filling sandbags and charts showing the above average rainfall hold her attention. Nobody confessed to taking the flood warnings too seriously at football tonight but Bingham's stores had obvious gaps on the shelves.

Soon the kitchen windows, dark against the night sky, collect droplets of condensation from the pans bubbling on the stove.

Will there be a flood? The Swan has small, framed black and white photographs of people standing arms folded on their door steps watching a flow of water race past their front doors, hens perched along the edge of a hay cart, ducks swimming on the village green. But that belonged to a different time, to a time just post-war when nature was somehow writ larger, did not know its place.

But it might be well to be cautious. Their row of stone-built workers' cottages is robust, not unlike the landscape where rocks protrude like knuckles through the thin-skinned turf. Water might sweep all away before it – pushing out doors and windows, displacing heavy furniture, scattering those small but precious human tokens, but the houses would stay. Olivia imagines the terrace, empty, mute, dripping, echoing.

She has come to love this small Cumbrian town spreading up the green valley sides, hinged by the fast river. They had found this cottage. The landlord was fair, either coming himself to effect repairs or sending someone in his stead. The rent hadn't increased much over the years. She suspected she and Zac were his *pro bono* case.

Zac had settled in school. His vowels became broader and broader as he grew taller and taller. She had found work in a solicitor's office and, by being careful with money, they got by.

Zac appears at the kitchen door, bare-chested, a long bath towel draped over his hips to the floor. "Go and put some clothes on!"

"Nah, I'm alright." He sits at the table.

Olivia shrugs and turns to the bubbling stew. "Aren't you frozen?" She notices a constellation of acne across his broadening shoulders. Some spots look raw and are weeping. He must have scuffed them when he towelled himself dry. He has the same curve of the back as his father. She wishes he would sit up.

"Nah."

"Suit yourself." This angular body of his, his sharp shoulder blades, this leanness all warn her to keep her distance. So be it.

She serves up dinner. Baked potato, ham hock, leek and white bean stew, vegetables from the allotment. She knows he's looking for black eyes in the potato, mini slugs in the leeks. It's decent food, lad. It's a square meal. It might not be what all your mates are having...

His chewing is noisy, tortured. She watches him for a moment. Mightn't she just stand up and tip his plate into his lap? That would teach him to be so particular. As if she would. Would she?

"What you laughing at?" She looks up at Zac. He is holding his spoon midway. The look of amusement brightens his face. "What's funny, Mum?"

His eyes are sparkling, his ready smile showing his chipped front tooth. Tip, it would go, the bowl. Straight into his lap. "Nothing. I was just imagining…"

Zac focuses back on his supper. "You're just weird."

"Ah!" She starts to protest.

"This isn't bad, by the way." He points to his food with the bowl of his clenched spoon. "Thanks, Mum."

A loud hammering on the front door interrupts their meal. "Who's that?"

"Well, there's only one way to find out, Mum."

"Of course."

"Do you want me to go?"

"No. You're not dressed. I'll go."

She opens the door to their landlord. "Hadley! Come in." She looks past him into the darkness outside. His BMW is parked on the road, its lights shining through raindrops frantically dancing in the wind, wipers arcing across the windscreen. Wet leaves like fly posters stick to the side windows. The roar of the river and the howl of the wind in the trees seem almost primeval. She's glad to see him. "Go through to the kitchen. Do you want a cuppa?"

She follows him to the back of the house. Zac has stacked the bowls by the sink and wiped the table. She casually tilts the lid of the bin to see if he has thrown away the remains of his food. Gratifyingly, he seems to have eaten it all.

"Aye. But only if you've got time. I don't want to disturb you if you're busy."

"No, we've just finished eating."

She fills the kettle but has to stop the draw of water because she can't hear what Hadley is saying. "I've just been going round the properties. Making sure everyone is safe."

"Safe? Why? Do you think the storm's going to get worse?"

"Well. I don't want to worry you but these properties in particular might be at risk…if the river breaks."

"There hasn't been a flood here for years, surely?"

"Exactly."

"Right. So what do you think we should do?"

"Sit tight for now. It depends what happens overnight. The reservoirs upstream are close to overflowing. The becks that normally flow into the river might not be able to hold the volume of rainwater and run-off. It just depends how the water gets channelled. I think we're in with a chance if it stops raining, but if it doesn't…"

"OK." Suddenly she feels frightened.

An orange light flashes repeatedly in the gloom. A siren sounds followed by an announcement. The words are slow but urgent. Hadley opens the front door. "Looks like the council and emergency services are out on alert." She follows him outside. There are wagons in the street, their lights flashing strobe-like against the fronts of the houses, up into the under branches of the trees along the river walk. Men in yellow jackets throw down sandbags onto the pavement. People, dark shadows, begin clutching them and dragging them like relief parcels. "Grab some," Hadley shouts above the clamour. "Patch the gaps under the gate and along the front door. I'll do the same round the back."

"Right-oh." The bags are enormously heavy. She can only manage one at a time. Someone puts a leaflet in her hand. Under the swaying street lamp, she just has time to read, "In the event of a flood…" before the wind whips it out of her wet hands. The wagons and the loud speaker move on to the next street.

Hadley appears round the corner. "You look absolutely drenched." She restates her offer of a cup of tea.

"You go in. I'm just going to take a look at the river."

"Wait. I'll come with you."

They cross the road that is shining like black vinyl. "Careful." Hadley takes her elbow as they jump over a bubbling grid onto the pavement. The street lights are dim after the brightness of the wagons and safety jackets. "Steps here." He braces her between himself and the metal rail as they make their way down the bank to the river's edge. Street lights above the old packhorse bridge waver in the wind, revealing the turgid brown water funnelling between its arches. They lean over the railings and watch the water racing like a primitive creature, its brown pelt scumbling, switching, peaking, backflowing. Olivia wants to lean in to the man.

"Come on. Let's get you in."

They step back over the debris of shaken trees towards the house. A car alarm is sounding in the next street. At the front door Hadley takes off his jacket and shakes it in the porch. His shirt is wet and shows his skin beneath. She hands him a towel from the ironing on the stairs.

"I'll go and put the kettle on."

"No. Don't bother."

"Oh?" The situation suddenly seems a lot more shocking if she has to face it alone.

"Where's that lad of yours?"

"Probably locked into his Xbox, oblivious to what's going on."

"It's just that I need to check on a couple of other places."

"Absolutely." She puts out her hand for the towel and opens the front door. "Go safely." Hadley steps over the threshold and shrugs on his coat.

"Shall I call back later?"

"If it's no trouble."

"None at all. And you can give me a bowl of that stew that smells so good too."

"Hah! Of course."

She watches him drive away before returning to the kitchen and turning the sound up on the local news. A storm-ravaged reporter is shouting into his microphone. "A month's worth of rain has fallen in the past eighteen hours causing difficulties to traffic and daily life." There are shots of submerged cars, flooded fields, stranded cattle, firemen walking a canoe carrying an elderly gentleman and white bearded terrier along a flooded high street. "Now back to you, Sophie, in the studio."

"A very British weather event, then, Clive." The immaculate anchorwoman smirks. Olivia snaps off the TV with the remote.

What should she do? Just what *are* you supposed to do? Is it too early to start lifting the furniture and the carpets? She decides to let Zac be, not wanting to worry him. She goes round the ground floor, unplugging all the electrical items, filling empty plastic milk bottles with water and making a pile of dry goods to take upstairs as emergency rations. She carries these, along with the ironing and warm coats, upstairs.

Zac is lying on his bed. "What's going on, Mum?"

"Just a few precautions. In case the river floods."

"Cool." He returns his attention to the game's screen.

She sits and waits, hoping that Hadley will come back. If they had to leave, where would they go? Upstairs, to be rescued through a bedroom window? Could they climb onto the roof, if they had to? Or would they just leave through the front door as the press of water pushed it open? What if they got hit by submerged tree trunks curling and looping beneath the surface of water? Alarm rises within her.

"Don't be a fuckwit. Calm down," she tells herself and pours a glass of whisky, but leaves it undrunk on the kitchen counter.

The loud knock on the door makes her jump. "Oh, you've come back. Thank you. Thank you. Thank you," she whispers rushing down the hallway. She stands back to let Hadley in, this time not wishing to look out at the fury beyond.

"Jesus, it's blowy out here!"

"How – how is it?"

"Well, it's still raining and blowing a Force Six. Quite a few trees down. The river's completely up to the bridge now…"

"Oh goodness." Hadley glances over to her, perhaps catching a sense of her alarm.

"But it's holding fast and it's not breached the riverbank yet. High tide's at two o'clock this morning. That's the critical point. If we get past that then I reckon we'll be OK. The storm is moving east."

Olivia looks at the kitchen clock. Three hours to go. Oh merciful Lord, please protect us and keep us safe.

"Is there nowhere else you can go?"

"No, not really. I'd rather stay here, to be honest."

"Good girl. Now, where's that stew you promised me?"

"Please, sit." Olivia relights the gas stove. Her hands tremble slightly as she works her way round the kitchen. There might be menace and danger ahead. The river is in spate. There is a charge, an intensity to the driven rain as if its purpose is to saturate, to drown. This airborne water is joining forces with water surging through the drains and the gullies, the becks and the rivers. Even the stew, bubbling lazily on the stovetop, is sending up traitorous plumes of steam into the already damp and laden air.

Hadley puts his phone face-down on the table and reaches for the bread knife she put on the table alongside the large cottage loaf. Does he need to cancel supper elsewhere to eat here? He carves large slices from the loaf and butters them thickly with the end of the bread knife.

"This is delicious," he mutters, his mouth full of bread.

If he does live with someone, she thinks to herself, they are possibly less concerned about table etiquette. A picture of her mother, Sorcha, flashes into her mind, her mouth pursed in disapproval. The image arrives with the force and intrusion of a thunderbolt.

"Glad you like it. I get it from Priunowski's. You know, the Polish baker up on Dent Street." Hadley shrugs, as if domestic details such as the daily bread are beyond his concern. "You should go there. Fabulous bread. Walnut and Caraway is my favourite but he only makes it in small batches, so you have to be quick." Hadley nods, his eyes flickering to his mobile as it buzzes and flashes. "Their Cheese and Garlic is also pretty stupendous. Have you tried the smoked butter from that place down by the quayside? You know..." Her voice trails off as he picks up his phone and punches in a short message. Shut up, stupid, she chastises herself, turning back to the stovetop to stir the stew.

"Here you are." She puts a large bowl of stew in front of him and hands him a spoon before sitting down with her hands in her lap. He saws away at the loaf again. It's nearly all gone.

What clues are there about this man? Crisp white shirt, ironed, frayed cuffs. A large gold watch on his right wrist. Is he left-handed? It's heavy and clunky and he twists the face round periodically. Her eyes flicker to his face. Broad. High cheekbones. Dark hair, greying. Full mouth. In fact, razor-sharp, straight cheekbones. Eyes – not much on show. A cleft in his chin. He is gripping his spoon as if it were a wooden utensil rather than machined steel. A touch of the caveman about him?

"You not having any?"

"No. We ate earlier."

Hadley continues eating, dipping the butter-laden bread into the brown stew. Golden beads of butterfat float away into the gravy. Their eyes catch as he lifts another spoonful to his mouth. He winks and she bursts into laughter.

"We'll be alright. Don't worry, Olivia. Worse things happen at sea!"

"Oh?"

"Only joking. Would you mind passing the salt, please?"

He eats covertly, bending low to his spoon as if guarding his food. His shirt speckles with splashes of gravy. He seems to be taking great pleasure in her stew.

After his second bowl, she offers him a cup of tea.

"Only if you'll have one."

"OK."

They sit, the corner of the kitchen table between them, and talk.

Hadley tells her of his early life, youngest son of a fells farmer. One brother killed under the wheels of a potato harvester, the other brother – older by fifteen months – inheriting the lot. Father never got over the accident, possibly felt responsible. Died young. Mother in a nursing home in the town. "Definitely got a tile loose, that one. Doesn't recognise me. Calls me 'Our Mickey', which was my great-uncle. Married – once, never again. Glamorous piece. Dental nurse. Called herself Candi. After Candi Staton. Used to sing in a band. Never really did more than a few charity gigs but she might have made it into the big time if our Louis hadn't come along. She used to sing at The Ridge on a Friday night. Pub full of druggies and ex-cons. She'd play a session there and they'd go from a cage full of wild gibbons to all misty-eyed and ever so slightly in love with her by the end of the night. Used to worry for her but it was probably the safest venue of the lot."

"You not together any more?"

"No. Divorced six years ago. Sasha, our second, is fifteen

now. Lives with her mother but we see plenty of each other."

"I'm sorry."

"Why? No need. What about yourself?"

What can she say? Which version of herself should she give? Sassy, single-mother struggling against the odds to raise her son? Hostage to fortune? Lonely onlooker? Emotional gypsy?

"Oh. You know. The usual. Married in haste. Repented quickly enough. Fled the scene. Working hard to make ends meet." Hadley nods. "The usual old Nine to Five cliché."

"Was that one of your wife Cindi's songs?"

"Yes, as a matter of fact, it was. Practically her anthem." He pauses for a moment… "While I was busy loving every woman I can, allegedly."

"And were you?"

"Was I, Christ! She had to beat every man at what she imagined was their own game. Her dad was a player and that affected her. She used to pull on the evening gowns, the sequins, the long gloves and the big hair and seduce pretty well every man she could – virtually, if not in reality."

"Including you?"

"You could say that. Thwarted ambition I think it was with her. She was capable of so much more. A dangerous thing in some women."

"Talking of danger, do you think we should just go and check outside?"

"Stay here. I'll go and take a look."

Olivia sits at the kitchen table as if bolted to her seat. It has been a long time since she talked with any revealing intimacy to another person, let alone another man. Are they trading their life stories simply because the world might end tonight? Or feeling their way?

The front door opens and she listens for him. As instructed, she is exactly as when he left – seated, head bowed, waiting. It is now nearly two o'clock in the morning.

"The river's breached," he shouts through from the hallway. "Halfway up the slope. Still a couple of feet off the roadside." She hears the crack of his jacket as he shakes out the raindrops. Black. Suede, wasn't it? Obviously a favourite. Shiny in parts. One pocket flap tucked in, one out. Even with the water's edge advancing towards the house, she is not concerned. All will be well.

"You OK?" Hadley asks, filling the small space of the kitchen, pulling his chair out with a clatter. Olivia nods slightly. "Don't worry. We're at peak tide now. This is the worst it's going to get. By the morning, all this will be over." He places his hand over hers. His thumb strokes her thumb. She watches the rhythmic movement. It feels like this could go on for ever and ever. "Would you like me to stay till morning?" She nods.

She should pull her hand away. Stop this right away. But she watches mesmerised before her eyes flicker up to meet his. They smile. He pulls her close so she has to rise slightly off her chair. The corner of the table digs between her ribs. Her finger slides beneath the button seam of his shirt.

He kisses her as if looking for a love lost, his body bent to hers, his attention microscopic as their overlapping concentric rings of etiquette, probity, self-preservation collide and smash to the floor.

Like a fur or a tanned skin has been thrown about her, she feels totally covered, taken over by his dark animal smell – strange, musty, thrilling. The smell of desire. His kisses delve deeper and deeper, like an auger, bringing her own feelings of lust and desire spiralling upwards. She wants to climb his body as a leopard might climb a tree – engaging every claw and muscle and sinew.

Pressed together they move like grasses in a fast eddying stream. She moulds herself to match his movement; he twists and bends to her unspoken entreaties.

A cup smashes onto the kitchen floor. "God. You kiss like a fuckin' savage." Hadley looks at her in astonishment. They are both out of breath. There is blood on his lower lip.

"Just answering like with like," she mutters.

"Jeez," he whispers. "What time is it?"

"Three o'clock." Should he really be somewhere else? She doesn't want to be there to see the look of guilt fog his eyes as he reaches for his jacket and his excuses. "I just need to pop upstairs. Check on Zac." She runs up the stairs and peeks around his bedroom door. He is fast asleep, his clothes in an untidy pile by the bed. He must have got undressed under the duvet, a habit of his from early childhood. Had he shouted down goodnight? Possibly, when they were out looking at the swell in the river. She blows him a kiss and closes the door tight before tiptoeing downstairs preparing herself for the cruel farewell.

He has, indeed, gone. She was leaning her forearms over the kitchen sink, trying hard to quell a reflex to retch when she hears the front door click.

"River's going down." He speaks quietly, placing a bottle of wine on the table. "Thought I'd get this from the car while I was out there. Zac alright?"

"Yes, fine. I thought you'd...gone!"

"Er...no. Still here, plainly."

"I'll get some glasses."

"And the corkscrew."

"Sure." Olivia circles him widely. He opens the wine deftly and pours two large glasses of red wine. It smells delicious; but to accept the glass would be to advance to the next part of the game.

What danger lies ahead?

"Let's go through to the sitting room. It's warmer in there." Hadley follows her, carrying the glasses and bottle, while she throws some more logs on the fire.

They sit at opposite ends of the sofa, half turned, Hadley's arm stretching along the sofa back towards her. In the subdued light, she studies his hand just inches away. Both are silent although thousands of warnings and questions tornado around inside her mind. That kiss had been a cataclysm. A powerful, unstoppable, raging onrush of emotion. Of passion. An incendiary spark between them.

She takes a large mouthful of wine, the strong flavours like a starburst inside her head. Hadley is still, staring into his glass. He sighs quietly, deeply.

"Look…," she starts.

"Come here."

She doesn't move. A log shifts on the fire, sending sparks up the black chimney. The cat jumps down and saunters out of the room, its tail high. Outside all is quiet – the wind no longer howling, the telegraph wires no longer singing.

"Come here," he repeats, putting down his glass of wine before reaching for hers. She mutely hands it over. For the second time that night, he pulls her towards him, arranging her so that she straddles his outstretched legs. Their eyes are level, flickering from left to right, chasing. His fingers lace her hair and he blows on her face to move a stray curl, making her blink. He laughs and the wine on his breath and the rising smell of her warming passion flow through her with force. Stubble is breaking through on his chin and she wants to rasp her tongue on his face, bite his jaw, grasp him.

With a restlessness, she rises and dips in his lap, up and down, back and forth as together their fingers seek out his shirt buttons and the fastenings on her bra. Suddenly she is free. He grips both breasts, pushing them together, hungrily, greedily sucking, licking each nipple, biting, squeezing, in a frenzy. She pushes herself further and deeper into his mouth, seeking out the pain, the burn.

But, really she has only one quarry. She lifts up on her knees, "Show me. Show me. Let me see!" She is scrabbling to undo his zip. She can't reach. Hadley catches her wrists between the curled fingers of one hand and lifts her arms up high and back. She looks down between her glistening breasts, the firelight catching on glints of sweat, as he sheaths his penis between the fingers of his other hand. "Let me see," she urges. "I want…" as a desperate, howling yearning explodes inside her.

He grips the base of his penis. It is big, plentiful. She rocks towards him. He flicks her clit with the wide tip of his erection, each contact setting off a chain reaction inside her, teasing her, tantalising her. "I know what you want, you fucking sexy woman," he whispers as he lifts her higher and higher away from her quarry.

"Please…" He moves her black pants to one side before licking a finger and inserting it inside her. "No." No, this is not what she wants. "Please." He looks steadily into her eyes as he drops her arms and lowers her down. God, it hurts. They adjust and shift and angle to allow him in; it feels as if acid and sand are burning her cunt. It feels red raw. It feels so good.

They move together, curving and sliding their bodies. He obviously wants to come. She has already come a million times. She holds herself just so to allow his rapid thrusts, watching him intently as he spills himself inside her and pleasure peels his face wide open. It is all over. He holds her close and she traces the scratches beaded with dried blood across his shoulder.

They hold each other, semi-naked, in the firelight; silent, wordless. She reaches for a glass and drinks some wine before passing it to Hadley. He finishes it in one gulp. He looks troubled.

"Olivia…"

"Don't say anything."

"No. I have to. Er…there *is* someone."

"I know."

"You?"

"No. No one. Please. Hush. I don't need to know."

"I have to. I'm not…"

"A free agent?"

"Yes. No. No, I'm not."

"Don't tell me. I don't want to know." Such details don't matter. "Anyway. Get dressed and go. Zac will be getting up in an hour or so and I need to be at work by nine."

He places the gentlest kiss on her forehead before leaving. "This is too good." She nods and closes the door quietly behind him, listening as the car recedes down the street.

Chapter 25

September 2005

Olivia
Cumbria

Thirty-seven houses on the western side of town take the brunt of the river swell. The local TV coverage shows huddles of people standing about, pumps with engorged hoses emptying cellars and ground floors of cold brown sludge. Sorry trails of ruined furniture pass from hand to hand into Council trucks. Mud, sand and twigs underfoot.

Three days later, Hadley's picture appears in the free local newspaper alongside the headline, "Local Businesses Help Flood Victims." She reads that he has offered accommodation to those made homeless including, bizarrely, an Afghan refugee who had made a temporary stopover for himself in an old, stone smithy.

A few days later he texts. "Come for a drive up Brigg Scarr with me?"

He parks by a field gate. Black plastic wrapping catches in the spiny branches of the hawthorn hedge and flaps manically in the high wind. Low grey clouds hasten across the fellside. Fattening ewes with long tails and bright coloured smudges on their wool nibble at the grass between patches of snow.

"I saw your picture in the local paper. What's the story with the refugee?" Raindrops are falling on the windscreen; on the radio Neil Diamond learns how to love and learns how to lie. "I'm glad you got in touch, by the way." She smiles at him.

"Me too." Hadley reaches for her hand. "It seems that this young man, Hamid – he's about seventeen – was making his way to Birmingham. Since he left his home in Nangahar province about four years ago, he's been relying on smugglers and good fortune and his wits to get himself to the UK. According to his story, all three have let him down fairly spectacularly."

"Why? What happened?"

"He fled Afghanistan because his father was an informer for the local police and the Taleban got on to him. As the eldest son, he had to escape or risk kidnapping and being strapped up to an explosive device and sent on the long walk towards a US road block."

She stares at Hadley's face in profile as Hamid's tale unravels. How the sight of him pleases her.

"Poor lad's obviously traumatised. He says his visa application was turned down because the Home Office say he's over eighteen – and he plainly isn't – and that he's an economic migrant. Which is bullshit. He can't be sent back, his whole family is in ruins."

"So why here, why now?"

"So, it's taken him about four years to get here. He'd worked illegally in Iran and Turkey and camped out in Italy waiting for boats and trucks and cars to take him onwards. Finally he gets to the UK. He'd been living with a foster family on the North Wales coast when there was some allegation made against the wife by a fellow refugee also lodging with the family. They both get chucked out and take to the road. The other guy wants to go to Scotland but tells Hamid that they're both going to Birmingham. By the time Hamid realises he's been duped, he's halfway up the M6 in the back of a truck wedged between hundreds of cardboard boxes. He jumps out at our local service station and begins walking. He got frightened by the river flooding and sought refuge in the old smithy where he was rescued."

"Quite a story."

"Anyway, we're doing what we can. Got him somewhere to live, put him in touch with a local church group and organising some legal representation for him to see if we can't overthrow the Home Office's decision. We need to get him asylum on the basis of the violence in the province of origin and the degrading and inhuman treatment of his family."

They both stare ahead. The wind buffets the car. It is getting cold and dark.

"Listen. I'm sorry. I need to get back for Zac. He'll be home from school soon. I live on the end of a pretty short leash, I'm afraid."

"Yes. And so do I. I…"

"Ssssh. Remember. I don't want to know."

"Understood." Hadley turns in his seat and gazes fully into Olivia's eyes. It is the purest pleasure to be so close to him. "Kiss me first."

Olivia laughs. "A quick one. Or else we'll never get off this mountain!"

Later that evening, leaning against the chain-link fencing, watching Zac and the under-14's football team practice, she receives a text from Hadley. "Missing you." She sends a kiss back.

Chapter 26

April 2007

Olivia
Thurstaston, The Wirral

Everything in her mother, Sorcha's house is exquisitely beautiful. It is the home of a collector; a shrewd investor in silver, ceramics, furniture, paintings. Olivia walks around the house like a visitor at an exhibition, diffidently pushing open doors, standing on thresholds, looking in. From the bedroom door, she can see a very fine layer of dust over the bedside table. The silver backed hairbrushes and pill boxes don't shine. Even without the benefit of the dust, objects will have been lifted off and placed back where they have always been positioned. The house has been empty for a month. They will have to decide what to do with everything now. There are no photographs. Stuffed between the spines of the hand-tooled leather bound books are no childish drawings or cards. Possibly no love-tokens or keepsakes either.

She locks up the house, feeling impertinent for prying.

The April morning is cold, unkind to the handful of mourners who had arrived early and sought shelter from the keening wind against the church wall. Most of the faces she recognises – from the nursing home, the village, the Potters Guild. Zac is standing next to her, his thin white shirt flapping, his lips turning blue. On a different day, she might have scolded him for forgetting his jacket, but today's not the day. She rubs his long arms instead and whispers, "Not long now."

The vicar, standing beneath the arched stone doorway, holding on to the iron door ring to prevent it slamming and hymn sheets fluttering, looks to Olivia. "Just a couple of minutes. I'm sure they are on their way," she mouths. Crows rise in formation from the long spring grass, strafing her view of the white-headed daffodils, diagonally dissecting it like an Escher drawing. The Vicar looks displeased and shrugs, and the solitary bell above continues tolling.

Toby had drunk steadily throughout the family supper the previous evening, his face becoming more and more flushed, buttons straining across his belly. Rose had confided to her that he tended to go one of two ways when he'd been drinking. "It's either melancholia or manly bravado. Generally, I prefer the self-pity. This squaring up he does, usually to someone he outranks in terms of size or age, is far more pathetic in its own way."

As the supper had worn on, Zac leaned in to whisper, "Uncle Toby's in his cups again. Watch out."

"I know," Olivia whispered back. "Drunk and getting more dangerous by the minute." Together they watched as he leaned back on his chair, surveying the table beneath crossed brows. "Who's going to be in for it tonight do you think?"

"Well, it's got to be Jake. It's always Jake."

"Which is why he's rarely here."

Why was her brother, Toby, like this? "It's not as if he was particularly close to his mother. Think he hated her too, didn't he, like he seems to hate everyone around him?" Rose commented drily on her husband.

"Maybe that's why. No chance ever now of that poignant reconciliation. Gone forever that opportunity of listening graciously and gratefully while his mother humbly apologises for moulding him into an uptight, repressed, angry, love-deprived, drink-addled fuck-wit."

On their way to bed, they passed Toby sitting in the hotel lounge with a nearly empty bottle of Rioja glowing in the firelight. He ignored all their various calls goodnight.

She and Toby will have to go back to the house at some point to sort out Sorcha's affairs. She knows Toby doesn't want to and she has no wish to either. That house – a substantial Georgian building that always looked more like an institution than a family home. A battle-zone, marked out in no-go areas. Silent mealtimes, food eaten hurriedly, heads down. Very little communication beyond times tables and Latin declensions and warnings about how many biscuits she was eating. Sent to bed early. No family photographs or keepsakes or jokes.

She catches sight of Zac – fifteen, beautiful, confident, full of life. The contrast is extreme, could not be further. She thanks her lucky stars for the second chance he gives her. All the hurts and sleights rubbed away by her glorious son; compensation a million fold. Why can Toby not see that? Why cannot he see that his children – Jake and Alyssa – are his route to salvation, his escape from his past?

The vicar gestures brusquely to them all to enter the church and opens the weather-worn studded door. A gust of wind blows the hymn sheets across the floor. The organ starts playing.

Olivia takes her place in the front row. She can almost touch the coffin. The air is cold within the church and people pull their coats about them while a chorister sings a medieval chant from the stalls at the back. The sound is pure and unwavering. A mist surrounds the coffin.

Sorcha had left no instructions regarding her funeral, other than to be buried in this hilltop churchyard next to John, her husband of fifty years. Olivia hopes that her mother would be pleased with the day's proceedings.

Toby rises to give the eulogy. It is a masterful delivery, she thinks, laying before the assembly a dutiful son's grief mingled with an air of confidence, not to say smugness, that he can be trusted – through the proper upbringing, the proper schooling, membership of the proper clubs and associations – to honour his family in the appropriate way. There is nothing of the discretionary tyrant in the slightly haltering voice or the almost undetectable tremor in his hands or the proudly uplifted head at the conclusion. Who could guess?

As she listens to Toby, Olivia wonders where her brother is truly to be found. Where is the carefree boy he might have been? Put out in the cold, granted, but why had he turned back to hammer at the family door rather than walk away like other members of her family had done, herself included? All except their dear old father? Daddy. Thoughtful, gracious, depressed. What *had* it been like being married to Sorcha for fifty years?

The congregation rises to sing a desultory hymn. Mouthing the words, she chides herself for being too cynical. Walk a mile in another's shoes first, perhaps.

The hymn is interminable and the organ squeaky. She can sense Zac becoming restless. He blows his nose before linking his arm in hers and whispers, "You alright, Mum?"

She nods. She is alright. She's fine.

The coffin is wheeled behind the vicar and his assistant, sun winking from the gold cross held high. As she leaves the pew to follow, she recalls the last time she saw Sorcha, only a few minutes after her death.

The nursing staff had told the family that Sorcha was entering the final phases. It had been a long day and sandwiches had been sent in for the family – Toby, his wife Rose, herself, Zac. Two nurses entered the room, one to clear away the supper things and draw the curtains partially on the descending dusk, the other to administer a dose. On leaving the room, the nurse had touched Toby on his shoulder and indicated that they should all draw near.

All afternoon, Sorcha had pulled her legs to her chest, slowly lowering them to the plastic sheeting, dislodging her blankets. Finally she was calm, her breath shallow and irregular. Toby stood, arms folded, observing from the window. She couldn't watch. For Sorcha, a woman forged and hardened by life, it seemed impossibly intrusive to watch the final surrender; too impossibly personal and intimate. Olivia left the room to stand alongside the empty tea things.

As the vicar intones over the lowering coffin, blackbirds and magpies hop closer and closer to the exposed earth.

"Funny how she'd bought the plot next door to John's grave. When was that? Two years before her own death? No way she was going to be chucked in on top and added as an 'And also…'" whispers Rose as the funeral director moves between the small group of attendants with stems of lilies to throw onto the casket.

The vicar's cassock is tossed by the winds, reminding Olivia of washing on a line. There is a faint roar of traffic from the motorway. The sound of a lorry reversing at the nearby do-it-yourself store.

"No. That would never do! Come on, tea and cake for us all." The small group processes over the tussocky grass back into the church. The vicar quickly removes his robes and stands next to a bubbling tea urn. He looks altogether more benign. Teetering towers of floral cups and saucers, the smell of lavender cake and hot water send a warm glow round the back of the church amongst the dusty hassocks and hymn books. "Funny how tea and cake bring you back down to earth."

"I thought that's just what we've been doing for Granny."

"You know what I mean, Zac."

Olivia stands to one side to allow people to get served before gathering in small clusters. A homely babble fills the air. The refreshments provide a sort of reassurance. Having seen off one of your own today, be content that it's not your turn yet. She thinks of the undertakers removing their ropes and planks, the sexton slicing the earth with his spade, filling the gaps, the invertebrates and bacteria beginning their long, long task. How final it all is. That really is it. She looks forward to a very different life now.

An elderly man comes to stand close to her. He looks reluctant to intrude, unsure.

"Hello. Thank you for coming today. My name's Olivia, Sorcha's daughter." They shake hands.

"I remember you."

"You do?"

"I don't suppose you will remember me. It was a long time ago when I knew Sorcha. I knew both your parents, actually. We were good friends for a while." His voice trails away, as if recollecting something painful. "I met you when you were… around fourteen, perhaps. And your brother, Toby. Except he was away at weekly boarding school, I believe."

"I'm sorry, I don't…"

"Paul. My name's Paul Frobisher. I met your mother when I was teaching at the Art Institute in Liverpool. She was enrolled in the pottery class."

"That was a long time ago. The seventies? That was the start of her career, her passion really. Were you one of her tutors?"

"No. I'm a painter. She helped me, enormously. They both did, both your parents, they were incredibly encouraging, both helped me enormously, in very different ways, at a particularly low point in my own life."

"Oh, I think I might know who you are now. Yes! Did you have a motorbike?"

"Ha, yes! At one time I did. I did come and visit your family. I'd moved away but was riding up to Scotland and called in. I remember you were sitting outside, reading a book. You seemed...I don't know...in a world of your own, shall we say?"

"I can remember the excitement. We didn't have many visitors. Don't think they were overly encouraged. But I remember the excitement when you turned up. Was that the last time you and my parents got together? I think I would have remembered future visits."

"Yes. It's to my eternal regret that we didn't meet up again. I corresponded with John for a period but, sadly, that's as far as it went."

He looks enquiringly into her eyes, silently interrogating her. Should she know more? Were there details of this friendship, at one time obviously important and original, that she had once picked up on as a child and then forgotten? "Excuse me. It's been a long journey." Paul moves to sit in one of the pews. He looks frail and old.

"I'll get you a cup of tea." Olivia returns to the counter. How strange it is to meet Paul. She examines her distant memory but cannot find much more than a few passing references to him.

"I'm afraid, thirty years ago nearly, I hurt your mother very much." She sits beside him on a pew, hands in her lap, head bowed, waiting for him to say more. He is pale and grey, elderly, colour and vitality all but faded away. "She had told me about a particular tragedy in her life. I was unthinking and careless and opened up old wounds. I should have been more careful of her feelings. And I think she thought I betrayed her by a prior friendship with your father that she didn't know about. She thought we were spying on her."

Paul's words come slowly. Each word is measured and polished before being delivered into her lap as if each word is a vital block to a confession honed over a long time. Olivia thinks back. So, had Paul been put beyond the bounds too? Tears flood her dry eyes and she cannot stop herself crying.

Moments later she is composed again. She looks round. Paul has gone. Did she hear him go? She regrets not saying goodbye. Beside her, on the pew, an exquisite painting which he must have left for her. A pile of boulders, the rocks picked out in all colours, beneath a blazing blue sky. On top of the rocks, a leopard proudly swings its tail.

Chapter 27

August 2015

Olivia
Wellington, New Zealand

The next day Zac and Aunty Joyce decide to take the ferry to Picton. Olivia is fatigued and stays behind. Before they leave, Joyce sits besides the orange crate that has kept its place on the sofa overnight. She pulls out a bundle of papers.

"There was a deal of unhappiness around the time Grace and Guy and your mother left Rhodesia. Unhappiness that greatly affected many people, and for many years to come."

Joyce stops, looking for a reaction from Olivia. "No. I didn't know that. Only that Mummy hated Rhodesia. She never went into detail other than saying she hated the heat and the termites."

"Your mother kept things closely guarded."

"You can say that again." A quick memory of silent mealtimes, the slow drag of empty time, long absences flashes into Olivia's mind.

"Fortunately I had a better rapport with Grace, your grandmother, than I did with Sorcha. Grace wrote to me shortly after Seb's death. I think she just wanted to unburden herself. She knew she could trust me, being so far away."

Joyce peers into the shallow box. Her voice is quiet. "There's a saying that it takes seven generations for a trauma to lose its effects on a family. I'm not sure I quite believe that but it goes some way to explaining how people become the..." Joyce pauses for a moment. "...the *black fruits* of a family. Your grandfather, Guy, had a towering temper. This possibly pushed Grace into a certain alliance. Your mother, too, was not unaffected by her father's tyranny. Nigel could never be sure if the decision was entirely his, at seventeen, to begin life anew here in New Zealand. Especially when it had hardly begun. I think Grace pushed him into it, for his own good, or safety."

She stops to look at her husband's photograph on the mantle. He returns a level stare. "It was a decision he never regretted." She smiles. "However it was arrived at. He was happy here. Had a chance to be his true self. He had a life of joy and contentment."

Lucky old Uncle Nige, Olivia thinks quietly to herself. The gifts of his life were not accorded to everyone in this family. What was the phrase Aunty Joyce used? Black fruits! Singed, scorched. A trace of lightning that ran from Guy – or from further back, possibly – spitting and flashing wherever his kinship ran. Certainly up to and including Toby.

"We'll leave you. Feel free, if you wish, to go through these papers. It may fill in some gaps in your understanding. Tell you something of your family history. Explain a few things. But then again, you might not feel the need. It's entirely up to you. We'll be back tonight."

"Bye, Mum." Zac gives her a kiss before straightening Joyce's collar tangled in the strap of her handbag. He turns back and waves comically before Joyce pretends to cuff him. They both climb into Zac's camper van and drive away.

Does she want to look in the box? Surely whatever is inside

concerns other people's stories, not her own. Why add to the misery?

Again, the image of members of her family being put beyond the bounds like so many rusting milk churns, standing in the mist, mute, isolated, unacknowledged, comes to mind. No one to know their story. No one to care. Grace, Guy, Nigel, Seb, Sorcha, John. Even Paul Frobisher, the artist. Why were their lives, unmourned and unremarked? Simply sufficient unto themselves, or do their lives have life still, in those still living?

She makes herself a cup of coffee and sits by the large window in the sitting room. It is cold, which seems appropriate if she is about to make acquaintance with some family ghosts.

The first item she pulls from the box is a single sheet of paper folded once. Her eyes fall to the word 'DEATH' in capital letters. It is a copy of a death certificate, a simple form filled out in a stranger's handwriting. 'Dead body found on Sixth July 1975 in Trebanog Farm, Hope Mountain.' Her hand flies to her mouth. "Oh, it's Uncle Seb," she says aloud to the empty room. Her eyes flitter, unsure whether she wants to know more.

The last time she saw Seb, he must have come to visit the family in Thurstaston. Magda was with him. What would she have been? Ten? She sees herself in serviceable trousers, clumpy shoes, a hand-knitted jumper, crudely chopped hair. How might Seb have seen her? The gauche, awkward, tongue-tied first daughter of his once-glamorous, now-timorous younger sister?

In a rather prissy, self-important voice, she might have told Uncle Seb, "We are not really supposed to talk to you, Mummy said." Did he have a beard? She thinks so. She thinks she can see a kind of gaunt face behind a mass of dark hair. What might he have said? What might Magda have said? For, surely, this small facsimile of her mother must have amused them both.

"Come on in. There's nothing to be afraid of."

Did she set foot over the edge into Seb's van?

"Mummy says you've got to sleep in the car port."

"Well, as this is your Mummy's house, we must do what she tells us."

Maybe she did step over the threshold? How glorious that would have been. She does remember underarm hair. Magda's. She had a lot of it, where Mummy had none. Seb was lying smoking against the van wall, an ashtray balanced on Magda's hip. Like Roy Harper reclining on a miscellany of tapestries, cushions, kilims, skins – the voice of a loving generation, peace and acceptance, Namaste. He later became the totem of her uncle. No wonder she was tongue-tied.

"Best go then, little girl, before your mother catches you."

Other girls might have sat prettily on the bottom step and chatted about this and that and then run merrily into the kitchen without censure. Other girls might have had their hair plaited into cornrows and sung clapping songs. So why was she always in the wrong? Coming back with the smell of marijuana in her hair and sent to her room for disobedience.

She must read on. She owes it to Uncle Seb. 'Occupation and usual address. Of: No fixed abode. Engineer and Inventor.' How sad. A remarkable man gone wrong. How terribly, terribly sad that he should be let go, unremembered, unimportant.

'Cause of death: Unascertainable. Found dead in farmhouse. Open Verdict.'

So, maybe he wasn't, as Joyce had suggested, murdered. But, maybe he was, and there was no evidence. Who will ever know? Who will ever care?

Did Mummy care? Did Mummy ever care about much? Her life lived behind a screen that blocked out any nuance or intimacy.

It was obvious that Daddy gave her pills to calm her down. She had those blank eyes. Olivia laughs out loud. Yes, it was the eyes.

Her memory shuttles to leaning back on the oven as Mummy squeezed her teenage spots between finely honed thumb nails. The need to feel her mother close to her, to smell her mother's breath, to feel her touch shames her as does the fact that this was the only intimacy they ever shared.

Eyes, again.

In her mind, her last touch of her Mother. After coming back in to the room in the nursing home, she stood beside the bed. "Shouldn't somebody close Mummy's eyes?" She had tried, lowering each eyelid in turn. Slowly and organically they unfurled, glassy eyes fixed upwards at the ceiling.

Even in this one small thing, she had failed – clumsy, wrong, indelicate, oafish, found wanting; belittled even in death.

But Mummy is gone now. And life is easier for that.

She pulls out a small book from the crate. *The Lonely*, by Paul Gallico. The book has a cheap, rough quality to it, the dust cover a hastily drawn sketch of a man's face and a woman's face, both melancholy.

Folded within its pages are several flimsy pages of writing paper. The writing is Grace's, recognisable from birthday and Christmas cards, but shaky and sketchy, that of an old person.

"This book is both a betrothal and a betrayal." The date at the top of the first page is 1976. Olivia looks for the date of the book – clearly produced in difficult times. Wartime or just post-war.

How can it be, as her grandmother described, both betrothal and betrayal?

Olivia unfolds the writing paper, slowly and tentatively. Are the silence and secrecy, witnesses to several lifetimes, about to be blown wide open?

"I loved Patrick. My airman." The word 'My' is underlined with a heavy, emphatic hand. "This is the book that brought us together. This is the book that excuses it all. Patrick was a child of the sky, like Jerry in this book. He sailed too close to Heaven (and Hell), called upon to destroy what he cherished – his world, his decency, himself, me. My daughter."

Olivia holds the book up to the window; the light is soft against the thick, mottled pages. Her eyes are tired and the printed words move about the page. She reads of bombs and rockets, boys failing to return, living with the ever-present chance of death. No chance to mourn or to remember. The superficiality of ritual in the time of war. Undisclosed grief.

The author's tone is didactic, heavily masculine and the language arcane. There are pencil markings in the margin. Words and phrases underlined, some manically. "Grief." "Ritual." "Wanderers." "War." "Superficial." A world of missions, briefings, take-offs, flak, interrogations, boredom and sleep. And a tentative romance between Jerry and Patches. The love story is old-fashioned, of another era.

Might this short tale of romance and unassuaged grief offer an explanation? For that male anger that roars like a flaming torch flung through the air and through time? Does the truth about her mother's years of drugged indifference, her slavish obsession to clay and cold-hearted hostility towards those closest to her emerge from these pages? Could they throw light on her own drinking and other compulsions? Uncle Seb's drug addiction? The brutality that Sorcha occasionally hinted of in her own parents', Grace and Guy's, lives? Toby's anger?

Is Patrick, Grace's airman, key to this family's silent drama?

A folded newspaper article shifts into sight. Olivia carefully unfolds the flimsy newssheet from the Liverpool Echo, dated 16

September 1978. One side is reporting on street riots and dockside strikes. A photograph on the other side contains elements from a more familiar world. Beneath the caption, "City Gallery Acquires Frobisher Painting," a face she recognises. "The Royston Gallery is proud to announce the purchase of this important painting by local artist, Paul Frobisher. The painting stands at over twenty feet tall and documents the rise and rise of the city of Liverpool from the mud of the Mersey to its subsequent renewal from the devastation wrought by German bombers. The painting will stand as a monument to Liverpool's fallen and a testament to the city's indomitable spirit." Of course! This is the artist who had come to Sorcha's funeral seven or eight years ago and had apologised for hurting her so terribly.

Olivia scans the smudgy, indistinct photograph. Few features stand out. Possibly the windowless arches of St Luke's? The river. The Cunard building. A river of fire. Fire in the sky reflecting outbreaks of fire in city streets.

She is sure she had been taken to see the painting in the Art Academy. Mummy is standing off to one side. She seemed awkward in its presence, her hand to her mouth, stiff. She remembers leaning on Daddy's shoulder as he bent down in front of the huge section and pointed out its features.

In the newspaper cutting in her hand, the painting is fully assembled. There's an aircraft toppling out of the sky, following in the wake of scores of bombs raining down on the city. The plane is on fire and the airman is shrieking in terror.

Rituals of grief. Rituals of grief and the airman. Patrick. Grief remaining dangerously under lock and key, threatening to seep out under tightly closed barriers to infect and destroy all new life and all known life. Black fruit.

Does she have courage to read Grace's testimony further?

212

What more will she find?

Wherein lies the betrothal? Wherein lies the betrayal?

Does she want to put aside the thorns – thorns that surround and protect the mother that might also stick in the flesh of the daughter? But which mother and which daughter? Fire and ice both burn. The flaming brand of anger. And the ice-rimed thorns of a mother's hostility or indifference.

The honest answer is, she doesn't know.

Patrick, the airman, holds the key.

For now, she will leave it in his hands. She folds the loose pages and returns them to the book, returning the book to the crate and the crate to the other side of the room.

Chapter 28

August 2015

Olivia
Wellington, New Zealand

Zac and Olivia drive up Mount Victoria. The wind nearly snatches the car door out of her hand. It's her last day before returning home.

"Come on, Mum. Race you to the top." Zac climbs the path, jumping from rock to rock. He is light, springs in his heels. As he speeds ahead, she looks at his ankles, bare between garish trainers and skintight jogging bottoms. Happy to be simply racing up a hill in the buffeting wind. Happy to be measuring his speed against the gradient, his strength against the stormy air. He turns and takes small running steps backwards. She wants to cry out to him to keep away from the edge, to do up his coat, zip up his pockets in case his inhaler or money fall out. But he is way too old for that now. "Keep up!" he calls out, his voice snatched by the wind.

"I'm trying. I'm a bit more wind-resistant than you."

"Fat, you mean."

"Cheeky sod. Come here!"

"Come here yourself!"

"Don't worry. I will."

Zac turns and sprints to the top. She stops for a breather and sees him at the pinnacle, silhouetted against the fast-moving sky.

"Finally made it then, Mum. Puffed out!" She can't tell him that it was the sight of her precious only son – tall, handsome, happy – that had winded her like an electric bolt.

"Yeah. Knackered." She looks out over the bay.

"Come on then." Zac grabs her hand and starts running downhill. Her feet slip and slide over the stones. Hair fills her eyes; she cannot see where she is going. They seem to be running faster than the pull of gravity.

"Let go. Let go," she screams. "You're crazy." He slows down, spraying stones with a sideways slide.

"Not exactly fit, are you Mum!"

"As a Mum, I don't see it as my duty to be 'fit'. Merely try and stay alive." Zac smiles down on her before grabbing her in a headlock and knuckling the top of her skull. "God. Quite frankly, you're a bloody pain!"

"I know, but you love me."

"Mmmmm."

Joyce drives to the airport. Somehow Olivia has ended up in the back of the car, Zac appropriating the front passenger seat. "My legs are too long for the back." Hail is hitting the roof of the small car, falling with an almost vengeful intent. People rush through the Government quarter, coats and umbrellas lifted against the attack. Out in the bay, several cargo ships sit at anchor, above them planes lowering themselves from the sky towards the runway.

Joyce will take care of Zac, if he needs it, but her aunt is more enthusiastic about her great-nephew's travel plans than she is. "It will do him good. It's what all the young people do. Hire a van, head down south, indulge in some extreme sports." Olivia blanches and her insides twist in panic at the thought of her only son swinging across ravines, mountain biking along sheer-sided cliffs, camping in remote canyons. "You've just got to let him cut loose." Olivia nods, mouth clamped firmly against the rising bile.

For now, she must simply gaze on the back of his head, watching the tendons stiffen with each of Joyce's poorly executed manoeuvres. "Oh, stupid man. Hurry up," Joyce shouts through her side window made opaque by the sudden fall in temperature outside. A cyclist is changing lanes. Zac takes the opportunity of her distraction to turn up the demister dial, flashing her a thumbs-up in the back. If they drive like this in the city, she thinks, how will he fare on the open road? Is it too late now to hang a St Christopher on his rear-view mirror?

The wet tarmac of the airport car park is drying in large, uneven patches, the invigorating smell mixing with stale aviation fuel. She stands by as Zac lifts her suitcase from the boot. How close they are to that tipping point where he becomes the undisputed adult and she becomes the dependent!

"Listen, Zac. We'll say goodbye here. No point you hanging around. The flight's not for a couple of hours. You go off."

Zac looks down at her, both relief and disappointment showing on his face. "You sure?"

"Yes. I think if I had to count down the minutes before I leave you behind, I'd end up a pretty undignified mess." Joyce is nodding agreement and gives her an unceremonious hug, as if bidding her to keep her emotions in check. "Thank you, Joyce. And look out for the lad here."

"You know I will. Have a good flight." She slips from Olivia's arms and walks diplomatically round to the far side of the car, out of range.

*

The plane is bound for Abu Dhabi, an eleven-hour flight away. They are flying into the night. Her fellow passengers are shuffling and organising themselves like roosting birds. Here and there, seat-back screens glimmer and flash with advertisements and sitcoms. There is little else to connect her to the earth below.

The drowsy hum of the plane is broken by the loud beeping of the seat belt signs. The cabin crew and those standing in the aisle stumble as the plane hits a patch of turbulence. Olivia feels her insides drop heavily into her pelvis and the jolt pushes air out of her open mouth. The reassuring voice of the captain tells the passengers that there is nothing to be alarmed about, simply the normal difference in air pressure experienced when flying over the Himalayas. She would just have to trust that the captain is telling the truth and dampen down the rising sense of panic. She looks about her fellow passengers. Most seem oblivious to the jumpiness of the plane although one or two worry their bottom lips or stare fixedly at the flashing lights on the plane's wings.

Olivia accepts a glass of wine from the cabin steward, deciding to drink it quickly and try to sleep. Various passengers emerge one by one from the toilets dressed in pyjamas, carrying toilet bags. She won't bother. She will have a shower, as hot as she can bear, when she gets home.

The wine is cheap and burns as it goes down. Here's to all the children of the sky and the wanderers in her family. May they find peace. And leave us in peace.

Olivia puts her head back and closes her eyes, setting herself the task of losing at least an hour or two of the flight in oblivion.

She hopes Hadley will be able to get away and be waiting for her at the airport.

Author's Note

Although *Children of the Sky* follows a map set out by certain members of my family, this is by no means a family biography.

Writing this book was inspired by a visit to the splendid little bookshop in Clare, Suffolk and picking up a copy of *The Lonely* by Paul Gallico. Gallico's *Snow Goose* was one of the first books I remember reading as a child. It lifted me off the page and into another dimension – that of imagination. To this day, I remember the jolt of take-off. Words no longer flowed in an inconstant stream before my young eyes. Words became spells.

So, when I saw a copy of this humble-looking book in the shop, it reminded me of that contract between author and reader. To tell a story, but with meaning.

The meaning behind *Children of the Sky*, that the ripples of trauma – individual or global – can reach outwards and onwards into successive generations if the rituals of grief are not learned and learned well, came from my reading of *The Lonely*.

This book is dedicated to all those who live between worlds, the wanderers who cannot find their homes, the Children of the Sky. We all know who they are.

Acknowledgements

Firstly, thanks are due to you, dear reader, for taking a chance on this book. Thank you – for engaging with the story, allowing it into your space. Thank you – for taking a chance on an independent author, for not selecting your next read from supermarket shelves or bestseller lists.

Independent authors are like your artisan cheese or beer producers. We can offer you great delights but we rely on reviews and recommendations to get noticed.

So, Adopt an Author today. Go along to my webpage, www.fionaholland.co.uk, for some free short stories to download and read with your cuppa. Click 'Like' on my Facebook page for news of upcoming events. Leave a review on Amazon. Please.

Be proud to be independent.

Further thanks are due to my fellow writers at Hawarden Ink and Hope Community Library for their generous support and feedback in the process of writing this novel.

Before All Else

Fiona Holland is also the author of *Before All Else*, a poignant and bitter-sweet look at a year in the lives of a Suffolk village.

Praise for *Before All Else*

Red magazine calls it "perfectly pitched".

"Initially it reads as a chatty, amusing, accessible view of the world, but the outstanding level of observation, the beauty of the natural description, and the insight afforded into human nature keeps revealing the literary prowess of the writer."

"So good I read it twice."

Before All Else is available from all good booksellers and online.

Find Fiona Holland on:
www.fionaholland.co.uk

Facebook: @fionahollandauthor
Twitter: Fiona Holland @FHollandAuthor